They sat for a long time, watching the fire together, and then finally Ethan reached up, his fingers brushing her cheek.

If he took it slow, then she'd have the chance to stop him at any time. But then Kate preempted that by stretching up and planting a kiss on the side of his mouth.

So soft. So very sweet, and yet with all the promise of something that might break the both of them if they gave in to it. Ethan wasn't someone who usually courted danger, but now the risk heightened the pleasure.

His hand moved to the back of her head, and he did what he'd been wanting to do for a long time. He kissed her properly.

As soon as her lips had touched his, Kate knew that this was a risk. But despite all that, she wanted him to kiss her more than she wanted to breathe.

When he did, it was a wild voyage, discovering a forgotten pleasure. Finding that she'd been wrong when she'd thought that one kiss couldn't possibly send shimmers racing through her body, making her fingers tremble and her toes curl. It was breathless, heart-pounding joy.

"I've been thinking about doing that for a while." He whispered the words, close to her ear, although even if he'd screamed them no one would have heard. Kate bunched the front of his jacket tight in her fingers.

"Tell me you're not planning on making me wait so long for the next one…"

Dear Reader,

People who've known me awhile often ask why I have dogs in my books. Let me explain why that's a very good question.

As a small child, I was terrified of dogs. It was a fear that I learned to control over the years but never left me, until one day when I was in my early twenties. After some hard deliberation, I summoned up the courage to ask a blind lady I knew whether I might touch her guide dog. It was the first time I'd been bold enough to reach out toward a dog, and it changed everything for me. Learning how to make friends with that gentle, placid creature was just the start of a long road, but I'll always remember the joy and achievement I felt.

Of course, like all irrational fears, this one is deeply irrational. Even now a tiny dog can give me a little start of alarm, and yet I'll bend down and stroke a large dog with gentle eyes. Like people, every dog is different.

So what of the dogs in this book? For me, Jeff, Arthur and Maisie are a tribute to the sweet-tempered dogs who helped a little girl get over her fear. It's a love affair that's had more than its share of ups and downs, but in common with Ethan and Kate's story, it has a happy ending.

Thank you for reading Ethan and Kate's story. I'm always thrilled to hear from readers, and you can contact me via my website at annieclaydon.com.

Annie x

HEALED BY THE SINGLE DAD DOC

ANNIE CLAYDON

HARLEQUIN® MEDICAL ROMANCE™

Recycling programs for this product may not exist in your area.

ISBN-13: 978-1-335-66336-8

Healed by the Single Dad Doc

First North American Publication 2018

This edition published by arrangement with Harlequin Books S.A.

For questions and comments about the quality of this book, please contact us at CustomerService@Harlequin.com.

Printed in U.S.A.

Books by Annie Claydon

Harlequin Medical Romance

Stranded in His Arms

Rescued by Dr. Rafe
Saved by the Single Dad

The Doctor She'd Never Forget
Discovering Dr. Riley
The Doctor's Diamond Proposal
English Rose for the Sicilian Doc
Saving Baby Amy
Forbidden Night with the Duke

Visit the Author Profile page
at Harlequin.com for more titles.

To Kate. Wishing you unicorns.

Praise for
Annie Claydon

"This is such a beautiful story filled with lots of emotion as two people get a second chance at love and one that is so well deserved."

—*Goodreads* on
Rescued by Dr. Rafe

CHAPTER ONE

DR ETHAN CONWAY WAS no stranger to the saving of lives. And also no stranger to the desolate feeling of having to accept that sometimes there is nothing that can be done.

And Jeff wasn't 'just' a dog. He was Ethan's dog. The gentle, giant Newfoundland would be over ninety now in human years. Old age was finally catching up with him and, if his gradual decline over the last three weeks hadn't come as any surprise, it had still been hard.

'All right, Jeff. She'll be here in a minute.' Ethan had parked the car in the empty forecourt of the veterinary surgery, and he twisted round in his seat. Jeff lifted his head slightly at the sound of his name and Ethan reached back, stroking the dog's head. Jeff had been with him for nine years, through love and loss, dreams and shattered hopes, and the thought of losing him now hurt.

It's okay to be upset about this.

The words of the pretty red-haired vet who'd seen Jeff last week sounded in Ethan's head. He'd explained to her that, in the scheme of things, this wasn't so bad and she'd cut through his bravado with one look.

Another car swung onto the forecourt, its headlights blinding him for a moment. It stopped at an interesting angle, taking up two parking spaces, and the driver's door opened. Kate Foster got out, hurrying across to where Ethan's car was parked.

'I'll straighten it up in a minute…' Ethan wound the driver's window down and she grinned at him. 'Have you been waiting long? I'm sorry, my last call took a bit longer than I anticipated.'

'I was early. And it's good of you to see us so late in the evening.'

She brushed the idea away with a wave of her hand, even though Ethan knew from his earlier conversation with the receptionist that Kate had been working all day. Despite that, she was all fresh-faced energy as she craned her neck through the window of his car, her gaze seeking Jeff out.

'Hello, Jeff. How are you doing, old boy?'

Jeff's tail thumped on the seat and he raised his head again. Kate smiled, and Ethan provided the answer to her question.

'He's been a lot more comfortable since you saw him last week. I've been giving him the medication regularly.'

She nodded. 'Good. Let's get him inside and I'll take a look at him.'

Kate unlocked the main door of the surgery and waited while Ethan unclipped the car safety-harness. Jeff lumbered slowly inside. The door slammed behind them and she squeezed past him in the narrow entranceway, leaving a scent of fresh air and flowers behind her as she walked through the darkened reception area and opened a door to the surgery at the back, flipping on the light.

'Bring him through…' She held the door open and Ethan bent, ready to lift the large dog up onto the examination couch. 'That's okay. Sit down there with him. He didn't much like it up on the couch last time, did he?'

She'd only seen Jeff once before but she remembered. Ethan sat down gratefully on the long vinyl-covered bench which ran along one wall of the surgery, and Jeff sprawled on the floor next to him, leaning against Ethan's legs.

'You'll be okay there for a moment? I've got to go and get my bag from the car.' She gave a smiling shrug that, for one moment, dispelled the weight in his heart. 'I should probably take another shot at that parking bay, too. I'm told the white lines are there for a reason.'

'We'll be fine. Call me if you need someone to wave you in to your space.'

She chuckled, and it occurred to Ethan that parking in a straight line wasn't much in Kate's nature. At work, she was thoughtful and methodical, but everything else she did betrayed a deliciously free spirit.

He heard the sound of the front door closing behind her. Then silence, broken only by the faint whisper of a car engine. A dull thud, and then silence again.

'Better go and see if she needs some help, Jeff.' Ethan shifted Jeff to one side a little and got to his feet. As he did so, the sound of a scream made the hairs on the back of his neck stand on end.

No… Not so much a scream as a battle cry—the incoherent noise of blind effort and determination. Ethan ran to the front door, cursing as he fumbled with the catch in the darkness.

His eyes strained against the shadows cast by the high hedge which ran around the forecourt. Kate's car had been backed into a parking space, and a few feet away she was struggling to escape from a dark form which was gripping her arm.

'Hey! Let go of her!' Ethan hollered at the

top of his lungs and the shadow froze for a moment. That moment was just enough for Kate to land a punch, and as the man's head snapped around his hood fell from across his face and Ethan saw him.

Young—early twenties, probably. Dark hair cut short. The details registered automatically in the back of Ethan's mind as he made a charge towards them, a roar escaping from his lips.

The more she fought, the greater danger there was of her being hurt. But instinct had taken over and Kate was fighting. She aimed another punch at the man and he threw her to the ground. Ethan heard Kate yelp as the man aimed a kick at her ribs, before running out of the forecourt and across the road.

'Kate...' She was halfway to her feet, scrambling backwards away from him as Ethan slowed his pace, walking towards her. 'Kate, it's all right.'

His words weren't registering. He'd seen this before, someone so frightened that they'd fight anyone off, even the people who came to help them. Ethan held his hands up in a gesture of surrender, his heart pounding.

She was stumbling towards her car, her eyes wide in the darkness, red corkscrew curls of hair escaping from the knot at the back of her head. Ethan tried to head her off, wondering whether she might be about to lock herself in her car and try to drive away, but she seemed more interested in the back of the vehicle than the driver's door.

'It's okay, Kate. He's gone now.'

'Gone?' The one word seemed to penetrate her panic. 'You're sure?'

'Yes, I saw him run across the road and get into a van. They've driven away.' He stepped forward and she practically fell into his arms, hugging him.

He could feel her body shaking against his. Ethan held her tight. This was…

It was almost…good. Almost the best thing he'd done in a long time. He smoothed the dishevelled curls on the back of her head, trying to focus on what he was supposed to be doing. Comfort. That was right.

'You've had a shock.' Ethan swallowed down the impulse to tell her that everything was all right now. However much he wanted to make it all right, that wasn't in his power. 'Are you hurt?'

'No, I…' He could feel her hands clutching at his sweater. 'I don't think so.'

'We'll get you inside and have a look.' He made to lead her towards the front door of the surgery, but she resisted, suddenly breaking free of him.

'Sorry…sorry, I'm okay. I have to get my bag.' Kate looked up at him apologetically, wiping the sleeve of her jacket across her tear-stained face. Flipping the car remote, she opened the boot, pushing a rug back to reveal a boot safe.

She sorted through her keys, pushing out a sharp breath as if to steady herself. But when she tried to open the safe, her hands were shaking too much.

'Let me.' Ethan held out his hand and for a moment panic flared in her eyes again and she gripped her keys tightly.

'Yes… Sorry. Thanks.' She handed the keys over and he opened the boot safe. Inside, he saw a small zipped bag which obviously held the drugs that she had been carrying.

He wished she'd stop apologising. And that she'd let him take her in his arms again so he could comfort her. He should tackle the first, as the second was a more selfish impulse.

'This was why you fought him?' Ethan put the bag into her hands and she clutched it to her chest, nodding.

'I know I should have just let him take the car but I couldn't bear to think that these would get into the wrong hands.'

She was twisting her mouth wryly, probably about to apologise again. Ethan cut her short.

'You might have been a little too brave, but

I can't say I would have done any different. I don't much like the thought of these getting onto the streets either.' He'd seen the results of that, more than once. And, if he couldn't entirely approve of a course of action that might result in Kate being hurt, he could understand her motives.

'And you shouted for help.' Ethan decided to concentrate on something that he could recommend entirely.

'I…was just making a noise. I didn't expect anyone to come. Thank you.' She looked up at him and smiled suddenly. *Really* smiled, as if he were some kind of hero, and not just a man who had a chequered and uncertain history of being there when he was needed.

'I'm just glad I was here to help.' Ethan took the risk of putting his arm loosely around her shoulders again, and she nestled against him as he shepherded her slowly towards the main door of the surgery.

He didn't seem to think anything of it. It was a big thing, running out of the surgery like that to help her. Ethan Conway was different from other men. Dependable, if ever she wanted to use that word again…

It was just the shock. The feeling that she wanted him to hold her and not let go would wear off, along with the tremor in her hands. He'd become just another guy, nicer to look at than most, but still easy to let go of.

But it seemed *he* wasn't letting go of her. He walked with her to the drugs cupboard, waiting while she negotiated the series of locks that kept it secure. Then back into the consulting room, where Jeff was dozing in exactly the same pose as when she'd left Ethan and him.

'I'll take a look at Jeff and then I should call the police.' Getting back to normal was what Kate needed to do now. She didn't want to think about Ethan's dark-blue eyes. Or the lilt of his accent, soft as the Yorkshire hills that could be seen from almost every part of this town.

'No. I'll make you a cup of tea. Then *I'll* call the police.'

His suggestion sounded a lot better. But she'd already spent too much time wanting to lean on him. She didn't want to compound the problem by showing him that she was hurt.

'That's okay, I'll…' Kate could feel her arm throbbing, from the elbow to the tip of her thumb. 'Actually, a cup of tea might be really nice. Thank you.'

He raised his eyebrows at her sudden *volte face*. 'Sure you're all right?'

'Yes, fine. I'd just really like a cup of tea. There's a tea station behind the reception area.'

It would take him five minutes to make the tea and that would give Kate some time to inspect the damage. 'Milk and three sugars, please.'

He nodded. 'You feel dizzy?'

'No, I always take three sugars in my tea.' Kate looked up at him half-apologetically, and he nodded.

She waited until he'd closed the door to the surgery behind him and then carefully slipped her arm out of her jacket, rolling up the sleeve of her shirt. Her forearm was beginning to swell, and although the skin wasn't broken it was an angry red. Kate turned on the cold tap, wincing as she let the cool water pour over her arm.

She could move all of her fingers and her thumb. Kate might be more conversant with animal physiology but a fractured bone didn't look much different however many legs you had. This didn't look like a fracture, and the swelling would probably go down by morning.

'Don't tell anyone, right?' She whispered the words to Jeff as she carefully dabbed her arm dry with a tissue and rolled her sleeve back down. Sitting down next to him, she wriggled painfully into her jacket, and Jeff stretched, putting his head in her lap and drooling onto her trousers.

'Yes, I know. I just don't want any fuss.' She'd bet that Ethan *would* make a fuss, and she didn't want to feel how good it was to have him look after her.

He reappeared in the doorway, holding a cup of tea. Setting it down on her desk, he pulled the high-backed chair out. 'Sit here. Jeff will be all right for a moment.'

Kate stared at him. No doubt Jeff *would* be all right. It was her own reaction to Ethan's stubborn determination to look after her that she was worried about.

'I'm a doctor. You took a nasty fall just now, and when the guy ran he caught you in the ribs with his boot. I'd like to make sure you're okay.'

Damn it! When did doctors get to be blue-eyed, blond-haired handsome-hero material? Kate supposed that his profession must be in the notes that had been left on her desk somewhere, but at the moment she could barely think straight enough to remember her middle name.

'If you're thinking about telling me you're all right again, then you should consider the possibility that adrenaline has a way of keeping the body going while you fight or fly.'

He had a point. Maybe she should have shown him her arm, to divert his attention from her ribs. But it was too late for that now, and mentioning any new aches and pains would only draw this out even further. Kate walked over to her desk, sitting down with a bump and wincing as pain shot up her back.

Ethan's expression softened, and she tried to ignore the fact that the smile on his face was inspiring both confidence and an inappropriate wish to touch him. He pulled up a chair, sitting down opposite her.

'What hurt you just then?'

'My side. Where he kicked me.' She brushed her hand across the spot, trying not to react to the pain that shot up her arm.

'Okay. May I take a look?'

'What kind of doctor are you?' She made one last attempt at resistance.

'The kind that knows the difference between a bruise and a cracked rib.' He grinned at her. 'Actually, I'm a trauma surgeon, so I've seen a fair number of both.'

'Oh. Sorry.' Kate felt herself redden.

'That's okay. Actually, everything's okay, just in case you were thinking of apologising about anything else.'

This guy was a bloody dream. Relaxed, good-humoured, handsome. Her hero…

She had to get a grip. If she just did what needed to be done, one thing at a time, she'd be okay. *Just draw the lines and stay within them. Forget about everything else.* She slipped off her jacket and Ethan reached around to the spot she'd indicated, pulling her shirt up a little so he could see.

'Lean forward a little more… That's right.'

She felt the brush of his hands against her side. It had been a while since she'd shivered at a man's touch against her skin and now wasn't a good time to get reacquainted with the feeling. She squeezed her eyes closed, trying to imagine herself somewhere else.

'Take a deep breath. In…' She felt his fingers around her ribs. Kate filled her lungs with air and her head began to swim.

'Out…' His fingers moved higher. 'Just relax.'

Relax? Really?

'Favourite place?'

'What?' Kate was dimly aware that his gentle examination had stopped.

'Your favourite place. Mine's at the top of Summer Hill. Do you know it?'

'Yes, I know it.' It was beautiful there, the hillside stretching gently down to woodlands and fields, small villages in the distance. It was a lovely spot, but not Kate's favourite. Despite the fact that London had chewed her up and spat her out, she still loved the place.

'Sitting by the river, in London. At dusk, watching the lights come on along the Embankment.'

'What part of the Embankment?'

'I like… You know the part by the statue of Boudicca?' Kate could almost hear the buzz of the traffic and the quiet sound of the water. She felt calmer now, just imagining it.

'Yes, I know it. I've always rather liked the cast-iron lamp stands they have there. The ones with dolphins at the base.'

'Yes, they're great. You know London?'

'I studied down there. Deep breath.'

Kate obeyed him without thinking. She was leaning against him now, his hands splayed around her back and sides. Relaxed, almost in an embrace…

She sat up abruptly, the picture of home that had been so real in her head suddenly dissolving. Ethan smiled slowly.

'Gotcha.'

'So you did. You're satisfied now?'

He nodded. 'Yes. I don't feel any sign of broken ribs. You may well hurt in the morning, though. May I see your face?'

He was going to do this face to face now? Kate fixed her gaze on the far corner of the room, so as not to meet his. She felt Ethan's thumb on her brow, smoothing back her hair. She must look such a mess…

'Just a graze. You might have a bruise there tomorrow.'

When he spoke, her concentration broke,

and she looked at him. His face was a model of propriety, but his eyes… Those eyes would be wicked in any setting.

It was all in her own mind. A blue-eyed prince in shining armour. Someone who could chase away dragons and then gently inspect for any damage. It was beguiling.

'Okay…thanks.' Kate pulled the scrunchie out of her hair and coiled the mass of red curls back into a neat knot at the base of her neck. The everyday movement seemed to calm her a little.

'Anything else?'

'No. Thanks, there's nothing else.' Her arm hurt like crazy, but she needed this to end. Needed to get on to the next thing on her mental list of things to do after a mugging. 'We should call the police.'

'I'll go and call them now.' He stood up, pulling his phone from his pocket, easy and unhurried, as if there was nothing to worry about. Clearly he was planning to do it out of earshot.

'Thanks. I'll…drink my tea.'

Kate waited until he'd gone and stood, stretching her limbs, trying to shake off the feeling of numb dread that suddenly accompanied being alone. Jeff raised his head, his tail thumping on the floor, and Kate walked over to sit beside him and stroke his head.

'All right. Everything's all right, Jeff.'

But everything *wasn't* all right. She needed to stop being a victim and get back to doing her job.

'Kate… Run…' Mark had shouted the words and then taken off, running away from her down the deserted street.

One o'clock in the morning and she'd only had eyes for him, not noticing the two men lounging at the entrance to her local underground station.

But she hadn't been able to run. Her bag had been slung across her body and she'd felt it being pulled, the strap tightening around her. Someone had dragged at her arm, pulling her watch from her wrist.

She'd tried to scream then, but there had been a hand over her mouth. So frightened. She'd been so frightened.

'Be quiet.'

One of the men had held her from behind and the other had searched her, feeling her neck and hands for jewellery. Then he'd cut the strap of her bag and taken that.

That might have been the end of it. Kate had been praying they'd just take what they wanted and go. But they hadn't. She'd felt someone push her backwards, and in a moment of helpless terror she had known there was no way she could avert what was going to happen next.

She'd felt herself crash down the metal-edged stairs. Lying at the bottom, against the closed gates that led into the station, she'd sobbed for Mark—but he had already gone.

The sound of the door opening brought Kate back to the here and now, her heart thumping to the beat of memories that suddenly seemed new and raw again. Whatever had made her think that moving away would allow her to leave all that behind?

'Sorry. I didn't mean to make you jump.'

She wasn't aware that she *had* jumped. Just that the familiar feeling of dread was back again, threatening all she'd done to chase it away. Kate couldn't let it back in.

'I'm okay. Really. I just have to get back to normal.' She wasn't even sure what normal was at that moment. Her nerves were jangling with alarm, and she was acutely aware of every sound outside the window—even the cars, passing in the road outside, which normally went unnoticed.

'Sometimes *normal* doesn't quite hack it.' He spoke quietly and Kate realised that she must have snapped at him. She took a deep breath.

'I'm sorry. It's just a shock. I thought I'd be

safe here...' Kate pressed her lips together. Something about Ethan made it all too easy to talk.

'Safe?'

'I moved up to Yorkshire from London a couple of years ago. I reckoned it couldn't happen...' Kate shrugged. Of course street crime happened here. It just hadn't happened to her, and that had given her a false sense of security.

'Something like this happened to you in London? Were you hurt?' Not only did he make her want to talk, he listened as well, reading between the lines. It was a lethal combination.

'I... Look, I appreciate your concern, but I'm all right.' Kate hung her head, squeezing her eyes shut. Maybe he wouldn't see that she was crying. 'I know what to do next and I really need to just get past this. I don't want to talk about it any more.'

She felt the brush of something on her cheek. When she opened her eyes, Ethan was wiping a tear away with a tissue.

'Okay.' He gave her a smile. 'But I should warn you that closing your eyes builds up the pressure.'

Despite everything, Kate choked with laughter. 'That's your considered medical opinion, is it? That if I close my eyes my head will explode?'

'Risk averted.' He gave her cheek another dab with the tissue and handed her a fresh one.

She was trying so hard to get on top of this. And she wasn't giving herself any time to be hurt or frightened—just swallowing it all down, to a place where it could do the most harm. Her free spirit seemed crushed under the weight of it all.

But she clearly wanted him to back off, and she was probably right. Ethan had no qualms about tending to her injuries, but anything else… That was wandering into the realms of emotional support, and Kate would be better off looking for that elsewhere.

'When did the police say they'd be coming?' She'd dried her eyes and seemed more composed now.

'About another half hour. I'll wait with you.' He held up his hand to quiet her protests. 'They said they wanted to speak with me as well. I saw the guy's face.'

She nodded, and Ethan wondered whether Kate had. If so, she seemed intent on burying that as well.

'If you don't mind, I'd like to take a look at Jeff now.'

Actually, he did mind. She'd just had a frightening experience and she should be concentrating on herself. But, if Ethan couldn't calm her, it seemed that Jeff could. When she stroked his head she stopped shaking and a little colour returned to her cheeks.

'When you've finished your tea…'

CHAPTER TWO

ETHAN WOKE EARLY. There was something wrong about today and right from the start he felt off-balance.

His first thought wasn't for Jeff, sleeping peacefully in the dog basket in the conservatory. Nor was it for his son, Sam, who he could hear playing upstairs, driving his toy cars up and down the wall. It was for Kate.

She'd told him she was all right so many times, but he was pretty sure she wasn't. Perhaps she'd feel better this morning, but Ethan doubted it.

He picked up his phone and put it down again. If Kate had managed to get some sleep last night, she wouldn't welcome him waking her just to ask how she was. And Ethan doubted that he'd get any kind of meaningful answer. She'd just repeat the mantra she'd been using last night.

I'm okay.

For about fifteen minutes she *had* seemed okay. Ethan had let her examine Jeff and she'd suddenly snapped out of her shocked misery and into an easy, professional manner. For one moment, he'd envied Jeff her smile and then decided that whatever worked, worked.

Ethan could understand wanting to get on with life. When his wife had died eighteen months ago, his work had given him some relief. It was something that occupied his mind fully, temporarily driving away the pain and guilt.

Kate's not your responsibility.

That ought to be *his* mantra. Jenna's death had brought Ethan's own responsibilities into sharp focus. He'd let his wife down, too busy and too tired to notice that she was more than just a little under the weather, as she'd claimed. And now he had to concentrate all his energies on giving Sam the love he needed. If Kate's smile tempted him to forget that, then he had to turn away from it.

'Dad?'

Ethan turned to see Sam in the kitchen doorway. 'Hey, Sammy. Got my hug for me?'

Sam ran into his arms and Ethan hugged him tight. He'd promised his son this, during the dark days after Jenna had died. A hug every morning and one at night. Last night, he'd driven home as fast as he could, afraid that he wouldn't make it, but Sam had stayed awake, falling asleep in Ethan's arms almost as soon as he'd made good on his promise.

'Grandma said a lady was hurt by bad men. And you saved her.'

Ethan resisted the impulse to tell Sam that Grandma was exaggerating again. Didn't every kid need to know that his Dad was capable of chasing away the shadows?

'It was just one bad man. I shouted and he ran away.'

'But you saved her?' Sam gave him a deflated look.

'Yes, I saved her. What would you like for breakfast?' At the weekend, breakfast was their time, and Sam got to choose whatever he wanted.

'Bangers and mash!'

Ethan raised his eyebrows, and Sam cackled with laughter. It seemed his son was turning into a practical joker, and the ache of having no one to share this with tugged at his heart.

'Waffles!'

'Okay, waffles it is.' Ethan set Sam down on his feet before he could change his mind again. His phone rang and he glanced at it. An unrecognised number ruled out Kate, the hospital and his parents, and anyone else could leave a message.

* * *

Two hours later, Ethan presented himself at the police station. He was half an hour early for the appointment he'd made with the police officer who'd called him and he intended to use that time wisely. The officer at the desk didn't recognise him, and he supposed that his absence had seen some changes here.

'I'm Dr Conway. Inspector Graham is expecting me.'

'You're the duty doctor?' The officer at the desk shot him a look that wasn't wholly welcoming.

'No, worse luck.'

Ethan heard Mags Graham's voice coming from behind the partition that divided the waiting area from the officers working behind the desk. Then the entrance door opened and Mags beckoned him through, closing the door behind him and shaking his hand warmly.

'Waiting for the duty doctor, are you?' Ethan looked around him. There were a few familiar faces who nodded a greeting in his direction.

Mags rolled her eyes. 'This guy's not as quick as you used to be.'

'Brave man. I was always far too afraid of you to keep you waiting.'

'Like hell you were.' Mags chuckled, leading him upstairs to her office and gesturing towards a group of chairs which were arranged around a small table to one side of her desk.

'So, what can I do for you, Ethan?'

'I witnessed an attempted mugging last night.'

Mags nodded. 'Yes, I pulled the file. Kate Foster. You dashed to the rescue.'

Ethan ignored the part about rescuing. He'd feel happier if everyone would stop saying that. 'I'm a little concerned.' Ethan frowned. He'd spent most of the morning telling himself that he shouldn't be concerned about Kate.

'On the record? Or off?' Mags was giving him that look—the one that told Ethan she knew full well that there was something he wasn't planning to say.

'Off the record. I think that this isn't the first time that Kate's been attacked. She wouldn't talk about it last night and she seemed very intent on telling everyone that she was all right. I'm not so sure she is, though.'

That should do it. Keep a professional distance, report what you know and leave it at that.

'Right.' Mags frowned. 'I see from the notes that you insisted she be driven home last night.'

'I thought that was sensible.'

'Yes, it was. We would do that normally anyway, and I imagine you haven't forgotten that. Is there anything we don't know about the scope of the attack last night? Something you're keeping quiet about?'

'No, I'm just concerned for her.' There it was again. *Concern.* Ethan knew that Mags was justifiably proud of the station's record for supporting victims of crime. Kate had needed him last night, but this morning he should back off.

Mags leaned back in her chair, her brow furrowed in thought. 'I'm going to say this as a friend...'

'Sure.' The signs were clear. He was in for a dose of Mags's straight talking.

'It's not unusual for witnesses of a crime to feel very protective towards people they've seen attacked. It's a perfectly natural reaction.'

'I'm aware of that.' Ethan's words sounded sharper than he'd meant them to. Mags was only trying to help, and the truth was that he *did* feel protective towards Kate. Perhaps Mags was right, and it was all down to the sudden rush of emotion he'd felt when he'd heard her scream.

Mags leaned forward in her chair. 'Look, Ethan. If someone I cared about was in the hospital, I'd be the first one sitting in your office, looking for a bit of...clarity. And you'd be telling me what I'm about to tell you.'

'To butt out and let you do your job?'

Mags laughed. 'I was thinking of putting it much more nicely than that. We're expecting

Ms Foster any minute now, and she'll be seeing Laura, who's one of our best officers. My suggestion is that you wait and see her afterwards.'

Mags's perceptive gaze scanned his face for a moment, seeking out any clue that there was more to this than he'd told her already. Ethan was beginning to feel a little foolish.

'Thanks, I appreciate it. And I'm sorry if I'm overreacting.' He *was* overreacting. He'd seen senseless loss before and felt the tragedy of it. And somehow, when he'd least expected it, Kate's predicament had pushed all the wrong buttons.

'Nonsense. If everyone cared as much as you do, I'd be out of a job.' Mags smiled, seeming to consider the matter closed. 'Now, let's see the latest photo of Sam. I know there's one on your phone.'

And there were photos of Mags's two daughters in her desk drawer which Ethan wanted to see too. He should stop worrying about Kate and come to terms with the fact that what he felt was just a result of the circumstances they'd found themselves in last night.

The VIPER system meant that witnesses were protected from any contact with the person they were being asked to identify, using computer images instead of a traditional identification parade. Ethan had listened carefully to the instructions, as if this were the first time he was hearing them, and was sure of his choice. The young police officer who had been through the process with him left him in the interview room to wait, bringing him a cup of tea and the morning paper.

He drank the tea and pretended to read the paper. After ten minutes, the door of the interview room opened and Kate appeared, Mags standing behind her in the doorway.

She just hadn't been able to resist it. Mags had asked a couple of oblique questions about his love life over the photos of Sam, and Ethan had ignored the suggestion that it might be time to consider dating. Then she'd seen Kate, put two and two together and come up with five.

It was a perfectly reasonable mistake to make. If things had been different Ethan might well have asked Kate out for a coffee and seen where that led. But, if time had softened his grief over losing Jenna, it hadn't softened the feeling that he'd let her down. Or the resolve that his first and only priority had to be Sam now.

'They said you were waiting.' Kate's smile seemed brittle. And, even though the day was warm, she was wearing a thick sweater and jacket, as if to ward off some nameless chill.

Ethan's heart bumped in his chest. Maybe his worries hadn't been so illogical after all.

'Yes. I wondered if you'd like a coffee. From somewhere other than the police canteen.'

Kate shrugged. 'Don't you have something to do?'

Mags's thoughtful gaze was fixed on Kate. 'I'm afraid maybe he does. I won't keep him too long.'

Ethan swallowed down the impulse to tell Mags that he could think of nothing more important right now than taking Kate by the arm and marching her outside into the fresh air.

'What, Mags?'

'I'm sorry about this, but the duty doctor hasn't come yet, and I have a man in the cells who was looking a little under the weather when he came in and is getting worse by the minute. He's just shown the custody sergeant a bite on his leg.'

'Bite?' Kate turned to her suddenly.

'Yes. It's not a human bite. We don't know what it is; it looks a few days old. Ethan, I wouldn't ask, but...'

He didn't have any choice. Ethan opened his mouth to ask whether Kate might wait somewhere for him but she spoke first.

'I'm a vet. I've seen practically every kind of bite there is. *Had* quite a few of them.'

'I'm sure that Ethan can deal with it.' Mags hadn't seemed to notice that some of the colour had suddenly returned to Kate's cheeks and she stood a little straighter.

'I'd appreciate Kate's opinion.' He was rewarded by a smile that didn't seem quite as strained as the last one.

'Fair enough.' Mags shot Ethan a questioning look but didn't argue. 'I'll get the medical kit brought down.'

This morning had been horrible. Before the taxi had arrived to take her to the police station, Kate had walked around her cottage checking everything. Locks. Dripping taps. She'd pulled all the plugs out of their sockets and then walked around the cottage a second time. She hated herself for doing it, but she couldn't help it.

The identification hadn't been much better. All she'd really wanted to do was to put this behind her, but the gentle voice of the woman police officer who'd showed her a set of short videos on a computer screen had screamed *victim.* She'd assured Kate that she wouldn't come face to face with her assailant, and Kate had wanted to scream back that she wasn't afraid.

She wasn't afraid, at least not of the man last night. She was afraid of herself. That she'd allow the bad dreams, the routines repeated over and over again, to take over her life the way they had last time. She'd been able to hide that from everyone but herself, but being unable to step out of her own flat had almost ruined her career and shown her that Mark's promises about sticking with her had been just empty words.

But, somehow, seeing Ethan had calmed her. Maybe because his final words to her last night were that he had to go in order to see his son before he went to sleep. A son meant a partner. And a partner meant that Ethan was unavailable. She could count him as a friend without any fear that she'd be tempted to step over the line.

'You've done this before?' Ethan seemed to know his way around the police station, walking ahead of the two police officers who were accompanying them.

'Yes, I used to be on the police surgeon's call roster. I gave it up a couple of years ago, to spend more time with my son.'

'And you worked here?'

'Mostly.' He looked behind him, smiling at the woman police officer who'd popped her head around the door after Kate had finished her identification. 'Inspector Graham was so impressed by my abilities that she had me assigned here most of the time.'

'In your dreams. As a police officer, I have

a duty to protect the public, and keeping you from bothering anyone else seemed like the way to go.'

Ethan chuckled. The easy respect between the two was clear. He must be good at his job, and perhaps Kate would get the opportunity to watch and learn a little.

The man was lying on the platform bed in his cell, a couple of blankets covering him, the custody sergeant standing at his side. Ethan glanced at the name on the custody record and leaned over him.

'Gary, I'm Dr Conway. I hear you're not feeling well.'

Gary opened his eyes, shading them from the light with his hand. 'My head's splitting.'

Probably a hangover—he stank of alcohol—but it was as well to make sure.

'You were drinking last night?'

'Yeah. It's what got me in here.'

He glanced up at Mags and she nodded. It probably wasn't entirely the drink that had got Gary locked up for the night, but whatever else he'd done wasn't Ethan's business. He preferred to be the cog in the system that didn't have to make judgements about others.

'All right. Have you hit your head at all, or fallen?'

'Dunno. Don't remember. My leg hurts.'

'I'll take a look then. Is that okay?'

'Knock yourself out, mate.' Gary closed his eyes again, and warning bells began to ring at the back of Ethan's head. He would have preferred it if Gary had been screaming for attention, because this lacklustre disinterest in what was happening around him didn't bode well.

A glance over his shoulder told him that the custody sergeant was ready to step in if Gary started to kick. Kate was out of range, standing quietly in the corner of the cell. Taking the blankets from Gary's legs, Ethan carefully rolled up the leg of his sweat pants.

Underneath was a haphazardly applied dressing of plaster and a bandage. Ethan cut off the dressings and saw the deep gash on the man's leg.

'This is a bite?'

He felt, rather than saw, Kate move closer, looking at the wound carefully. 'I think that's from a lizard. Lizard bites sometimes bleed very freely.'

'This is deep.' Ethan gently felt the skin around the wound. It was swollen and hot to the touch.

Kate turned her attention to Gary, poking his shoulder. He opened his eyes and kept them open, clearly liking Kate's smile a little better than he did Ethan's. Who could blame him?

'Was it a lizard that bit you?'

'Great, big ugly thing with sharp teeth.'

'About this long?' She held out her hands to indicate something of about three and a half feet in length. 'Brownish colour with a light belly? Scales?'

'Yeah, scales. Quick on its feet as well. My mate bought it from somewhere.' The man closed his eyes again.

'It could be a monitor lizard. Their bites often don't hurt much at first, but give it twenty-four hours and they can become infected very quickly. If he's been drinking he probably didn't register the pain.' She turned to Ethan. It was a relief, but no particular surprise, to see that she was calm and collected. Almost welcoming the opportunity to do something which didn't revolve around last night.

'It's certainly infected.' Ethan took a surgical marker pen from the first-aid kit, drawing around the edge of the hard red lump that surrounded the bite, and noting the time so that any increase in the swelling could be monitored.

'You think we should call an ambulance?' Mags anticipated his next request.

'Yeah, this definitely needs to be looked at. I'll clean it and dress it to stop the bleeding.'

He looked up as a young man appeared in the doorway, holding a medical bag.

'Sorry I'm late. If I could take a look at the patient now—'

'This is Dr Conway,' Mags broke in. 'He's worked with us before.'

'Oh.' The young doctor looked flustered and more than a little put out. Ethan stood, holding out his hand.

'If I can fill you in on the details, maybe you can take things from here.'

'His face… If looks could kill.' Kate smiled up at him as they walked out of the police station.

Ethan shrugged. 'If he'd got to the patient first, I don't imagine he could have done any better. I personally thought my diagnosis of a lizard bite was quite inspired. And I made it so quickly!'

The look of smiling outrage that Kate shot at him was exactly what he'd been aiming for. '*Your* diagnosis?'

'Yeah. It was me that said lizard first, wasn't it?'

'I don't think so. What kind of lizard was it you had in mind again?'

Ethan chuckled. 'Oh, you know. One of the ones with teeth.'

'They're the ones you really don't want to bite you.'

'My thoughts exactly. And whoever *did* say lizard did a very fine job.'

He hadn't planned on this. Before he'd seen Kate this morning Ethan had managed to convince himself that Mags was right and that the urge to see Kate, which had escalated into need, was just a result of his having witnessed the attack on her last night. But now laughter was buzzing between them and all he wanted to do was put his arm around her. To try and make her forget the things that had made her so hollow-eyed when he'd first set eyes on her this morning. It was confusing.

She looked up and down the high street as if she wasn't quite sure which way to go. Then she smiled up at him. 'I'm just looking for the bus stop. The police still have my car. Apparently there are some fingerprints and fibres on it.'

'Can I give you a lift home?' Somehow, making the decision to stay rather than go made him feel better. Sam was occupied and with his grandparents. Why shouldn't he spend some time with Kate?

'Thanks, but I'm not going home.'

'Where are you going, then?'

Kate hesitated, as if that wasn't something she really wanted him to know. Ethan raised his eyebrows in a signal that he wasn't going to accept silence for an answer.

'Actually, I'm going to the hospital. My arm really hurts, and I thought I'd go to the minor injuries clinic.'

Ethan rejected the urge to ask her why on earth she hadn't mentioned this last night. 'I'll give you a lift there, then. We can pick up a coffee on the way, if you like.'

'They gave me some tea.'

'Me too. I need something to wash the taste away.' He grinned at her. 'And coffee from the vending machine at the hospital isn't going to do it.'

She laughed suddenly. 'Yes, okay then. Thanks, coffee and a lift would be great.'

'I can walk from here. It's only down the road.' Ethan had gone to fetch the coffee, and that had given Kate some time to think. It felt safe in his car, but that was only a temporary relief, and she had to get used to functioning on her own.

'It's Saturday, and there are bound to be queues at the minor injuries clinic. If they're too long I can take a look at your arm myself.' He settled back into the driver's seat.

No. Feeling safe with Ethan was one thing. Relying on him was something very different. And she had the perfect excuse.

'I'm sure your partner won't thank me for keeping you away for so long. Didn't you say that you gave up working at weekends to spend more time with your family?'

'With my son. My wife died eighteen months ago and it's just me and Sam now—' He broke off as Kate's hand flew to her mouth.

'Oh. I'm so sorry.'

He nodded, seeming almost as lost for words as she was. 'It's… I didn't intend to be so blunt. I just can't think of a more tactful way of saying it.'

Kate swallowed hard, suddenly wanting to take a large swig of the coffee he still held in his hand. A sugar rush would be good right now.

'It's up to you to say it however you want. What you and your son are comfortable with is what matters.'

Ethan smiled suddenly, nodding. 'Sam's the one who really matters.'

'Of course. And I'm sure he wants you home on a Saturday morning, doesn't he?'

'Not this morning. I took him over to my parents when I knew I was coming down to the police station, and they've promised him a trip to the adventure park. I doubt he'll appreciate me coming home too soon.'

It would be wiser to turn his offer down nicely and get out of the car. But Kate couldn't do it, not now. She reached for the cardboard beaker in his hand.

'Thank you. It's very kind of you.'

He grinned, reaching for the ignition, and then thinking better of it and leaning back in his seat, taking a sip from his own drink. 'My pleasure. Anyway, I'm intrigued to know whether you're actually going to drink that.'

Kate peeled the plastic top from her beaker, squinting at her drink. 'Why, what have you put in it?'

'Only what you asked for—an extra shot of espresso, whipped cream and caramel. Just one sugar, this time. It sounds…interesting.'

'Ah. So you're a "don't put flavours in my coffee" type, are you?' His medium-sized cup, alongside her large one, indicated that he probably was. Kate took a sip from her beaker and rolled her eyes in an expression of defiant bliss.

Ethan chuckled and started the car.

It had been a relief to tell Kate where he stood. Letting her know that Sam was the single most important thing in his life now and hearing her obvious acceptance of that had cleared away his doubts and allowed him to concentrate on the matter at hand.

A and E was crowded and so was the minor injuries clinic. Kate seemed to be sticking close by his side, nursing her arm against her chest, and Ethan reckoned it must be really hurting her. He decided on a quieter place, away from the noise and activity, and steered her towards the lift.

'This is your office?' She looked around as he opened the door and ushered her inside. 'It's very tidy.'

'I don't spend much time in here. Not much chance to make a mess.' Ethan wondered what Kate thought of the straight lines and utilitarian order. Her own surgery was neat and comfortable but one wall broke the pattern, an exuberant mass of photographs, obviously added piecemeal as and when people provided pictures of the animals she'd treated.

It was a sobering thought. Last night, her free spirit seemed to have been crushed under the weight of shock and distress. This morning, it was as if she was undergoing some internal struggle. He'd seen flashes of that delicious exuberance, but she was still frightened and bemused, still trying to cope by putting everything back in its proper place.

'Is this your son Sam?' She was looking at the framed photograph on his desk, tucked neatly behind the phone.

'Yes, that's him. He's five now.' The framed photograph was just over a year and a half old, the last one that Jenna had taken of him, and Ethan had stuck a more recent one of Sam in the corner of the frame.

'He's a beautiful little boy.' She was studying both photographs carefully. 'You must be very proud of him.'

'Yes, I am. He's got a great sense of humour, and he's kind.' Sam's dark hair and eyes were like Jenna's.

'Does he want to be a doctor when he grows up? Like his Dad?'

'No, he has bigger fish to fry. He wants to be a superhero and save the world.'

She gave a little laugh, putting the photograph back down again, tilting it carefully so that it was in the exact same place she'd found it. 'That's close enough to being a doctor, don't you think?'

Saving the world wasn't exactly Ethan's thing; he confined himself to doing the best he could. The photo on his desk was a reminder of that. Sam was smiling at his mother. They'd been a happy family. Two weeks later, Ethan had left for work, too hurried to do anything other than take Jenna's assurances that the urinary infection she had was a little better. That night he'd stayed at work and the following day Jenna had been taken into hospital. By that time, the sepsis had too tight a hold on her.

'Let's have a look at your arm, then.' He turned his mind to things that were still possible to change, watching as Kate pulled her jacket off painfully.

She got tangled in the sweater as she pulled it over her head, and he leaned forward to help. As he pulled it off her arm, she caught her breath in pain.

'That's really hurting you.'

She nodded, as if making a shameful admission. 'It does hurt a bit.'

'Let me see, then.' He gently rolled up the sleeve of her shirt. The arm was swollen from wrist to elbow, the skin bruised and inflamed.

'And you didn't notice this last night?' Ethan couldn't help the gentle reproach.

'It hurt a bit then, too.'

And she'd pretended that it was nothing, the same as Jenna had. The thought clawed at his heart.

'All right. I'm going to want an X-ray.'

'It's not broken.'

'Let me be the judge of that. You're in *my* surgery now.'

'Okay, doctor.'

Ethan smiled. He wasn't going to allow her to go until he was sure that she was physically all right, and it seemed that Kate was finally coming to accept that.

* * *

'There's no fracture, which is always good.' Kate had craned over his shoulder while he reviewed the X-rays, and Ethan had been momentarily blinded by her scent. Now that she was back in her seat he could think more clearly. He paused for a moment to admire the fine structure of her bones, and then forced his mind back to the matter at hand.

'You have some bruising there. He grabbed your arm?' Ethan avoided the very obvious fact that the bruising was in the shape of a handprint.

'Yes.' Kate twisted her other hand around, trying to demonstrate, but her thumb was on the opposite side from the handprint. Slowly, shyly, she held her arm out towards him.

Ethan felt something block his throat. Gently, he laid his fingers on her arm over the bruises. 'Like this?'

'Yes. Just like that.'

Her gaze met his. An unspoken message that somehow tenderness might wipe away the violence. His hand, placed in the exact spot her attacker's had been, might somehow heal her.

'Well there's some trauma, and it'll be painful for a while, but with rest it should improve in the next week or so. The bruising will fade eventually.' If he could have erased the bruises now, Ethan would have given almost anything to do so.

She nodded. Ethan wondered whether kissing it better would make any difference, the way he did with Sam's bumps and scrapes, and decided that was way out of his medical remit.

'Use ice packs to relieve the swelling. And I'm going to give you a sling.'

'But my work…' Alarm registered in her eyes.

'Maybe you should take some time off work. Just a few days, to get over the shock.'

She shook her head, pulling her arm away from his fingers and cradling it in her lap. 'I don't want to take time off work. I want things back to normal as soon as possible.'

'Are you sure you're not pushing yourself too hard?'

'Yes, I'm sure. This is what I want.'

There was no disagreeing with her. And, even if he could, perhaps Kate was right about this and he was wrong. But he could at least attend to her medical needs.

'In that case, I'm going to insist you wear the sling for a week. You need to keep that arm rested to allow it to heal.'

Kate nodded. 'All right. I can get one of the veterinary nurses to help me at work.'

This was a victory of sorts. Ethan hid his

smile, scribbling a note on his pad to send down to the dispensary. 'I'm going to prescribe some painkillers as well. Just enough for a few days. If you have significant pain after that, you should go and see your own doctor.'

'Thanks. I think I'll be wanting those.'

There was one more thing he had to ask. He didn't even want to think about it, but maybe it would be better coming from him.

'Have the police seen your injuries?' Ethan kept his eyes fixed on the pad in front of him, as if he were checking what he'd written and this was just an aside.

'No.'

When he glanced up at her, her cheeks were bright red. Ethan knew that the officer she'd seen would have asked about injuries, and Kate had probably repeated the mantra that she was okay. She'd probably turned down the offer of victim support as well.

'You know, don't you, that they've caught the man?' She nodded. 'And that they'll be wanting as much evidence against him as they can gather. It's up to you, of course.'

It was, technically, up to Kate. But Ethan had no doubt that there would be an attempt at persuasion. Maybe it was better coming from him.

'They'll want photographs, won't they? To show in court. They did that the last time.'

So she *had* been hurt before. It seemed to Ethan that Kate was fighting not just this incident but her memories of the last one.

'Yes, they will. As a medical practitioner, it's my duty to encourage you to report any injury that's the result of a crime. As a…friend, I'll tell you that this is a difficult process, but one that may well help you to feel better in the long run. It helps if you decide to do it on your own terms.'

She thought for a moment. Then that spark of resilience flashed in her eyes. 'Yes, you're right. Can you do it?'

The thought that she trusted *him* was almost overwhelming. Ethan could do it. He'd documented and photographed injuries many times before for police use. If there were any question about his personal involvement in the crime, then he'd take the flack that Mags would almost certainly dispense.

'You're sure?'

'Yes. Positive.' Now that Kate had made up her mind, she seemed impatient for action.

'All right. I'll go and get the forms and see if I can find a nurse.' An impartial observer would be good on two counts—first to countersign the forms. Mags would like that. And second to help Kate pull up her shirt at the back and position her arm. Because, if the first time he'd touched her had been intoxicating, now it was almost becoming a craving.

CHAPTER THREE

THIS WAS NOT GOOD. A hero, someone who would appear out of nowhere and save the day… It was every girl's dream, which was absolutely fine, just as long as that hero didn't think he could remove himself from the imaginary world and infiltrate reality.

And Ethan Conway was more than six feet of solid reality. The kind that made her melt when she looked at him and shiver whenever he touched her. He'd stepped out of a dream, and was wreaking havoc with her waking world, and she'd let him do it. She'd given in and allowed him to help her.

He'd been in the right place at the right time. That was all it was. If she could just concentrate on not being so needy, then Ethan wouldn't seem so much of a hero.

Kate had learned her lesson, the last time she'd been mugged. It had been two days before Mark had come to see her. Looking around and declaring that he hated hospitals, he'd dumped an ostentatious bunch of flowers across her legs, making Kate wince in pain, and then had selected a chair, brushed it off with a handkerchief and sat down.

After the attack, as soon as she'd been able to get someone to help her with the phone, Kate had made frantic calls, trying to find out whether Mark was all right. She'd heard that he was professing himself to be a bit shaken up, but that he was uninjured, and her friends had expressed surprise when they'd heard she was in hospital. Mark had never thought to mention that.

'It's every man for himself in these situations, Kate.' Mark had seemed keen to justify his actions, but suddenly guilt had cut into his air of nonchalance.

He couldn't have known. That was what Kate had been telling herself. He'd thought that she'd be able to run too, and that was why he hadn't come back. And afterwards…? Perhaps he'd felt guilty and that had kept him away.

Mark's mouth twisted suddenly. 'You need to keep your wits about you a bit more.'

'I… I couldn't get away…' Tears had blurred her vision and Kate had tried to blink them away. However needy she'd felt, however battered and bruised, it had been clear that Mark didn't want to see it.

'Like I said—if you'd been taking notice, then you would have been right behind me.'

Mark had shaken his head slowly, as if her slow-wittedness left him at a loss.

And that had been the end of it. Mark had talked about a film he'd gone to see—one that they'd been planning to see together—and had left exactly one hour after he'd arrived. He'd clearly been keeping his eye on the time.

She'd asked one of the nurses to give the flowers to a woman at the other end of the ward, who didn't seem to have any. Mark wasn't coming back.

And he'd been right in one thing. If Kate couldn't look after herself, then no one else would.

Kate stubbornly refused to call Ethan, and he hadn't called her. For three weeks she'd worked solidly, trying to get her life back into some semblance of normality. And then his name showed up on her caller display.

This must be the call she'd made him promise to make. She tapped the answer button, smiling into the phone, trying to inject some of that smile into her tone.

'Hi, Ethan. How's everything?'

'It's Jeff. He's failing fast.' His voice was broken with emotion.

'Okay. Why don't I drop in and see you? I've just finished my Friday evening surgery, and I can be with you in half an hour.'

'Are you sure? That would be great.'

'That's fine. No point in having you come all the way here.' If Ethan *was* going to lose Jeff tonight, then it would be better for both he and his dog if they were at home. Then a thought struck her.

'What about Sam? Is he there?'

'I've explained everything to him. He seems to be taking it better than I am...'

Ethan's voice faltered and Kate wished she could hug him. This must be so hard for him. Not only dealing with his own feelings but also trying to decide what was best for Sam.

'I'll call my mother and ask her to pick him up. He can spend the night with my parents. Perhaps we can take things from there?' Ethan seemed to pull himself together suddenly.

'Okay, that's a good idea. I'll see you soon.'

Kate ended the call and pulled on her jacket. Then she hurried outside to her car.

Ethan had hoped that Sam would be gone by the time that Kate arrived. But his son was dawdling, obviously waiting for something before he went with his grandmother, and Ethan didn't have the heart to hurry him up.

The doorbell rang, and Sam ran to the door with him. 'Why don't you go upstairs and help Grandma?' Ethan tried to deflect Sam but Sam shook his head stubbornly.

'No!' Sam pressed his face against the glass in the front door, trying to see through the frosted panels. Ethan saw movement outside, a blur of red hair and the wave of an arm. Sam waved back.

'Out of the way, then.' Sam stepped back a little, allowing Ethan to open the door.

'Hello.' Sam greeted Kate before Ethan had a chance to.

'Hello. You must be Sam.' Kate smiled down at his son and Sam nodded.

'Are you the lady who might take Jeff to heaven?'

Sam had clearly taken everything that Ethan had told him and put it together in his own way. Ethan flashed a look of apology at Kate, gently trying to move Sam away from the doorway.

Both of them ignored him. Kate bent down and Sam escaped his grip, joining her on the front porch.

'Yes, I am.' She reached out, brushing the back of Sam's hand with one finger. 'Is it all right with you if I come in?'

Sam looked Kate up and down, obviously thinking about it. Kate was smiling, and any interruption was suddenly impossible, as the two sized each other up.

'Dad says that Jeff's very, very old.'

'Yes, he is.' Kate's tone was gentle.

'Will he see Mummy in heaven?' Sam's question delivered a knife to Ethan's heart. He saw Kate's gaze flip up towards him, in the way that most people's did when Sam asked questions about his mother, but she didn't back off or change the subject, leaving Sam to wonder what was going on.

'What do you think, Sam?'

'He will.'

'I think you're right.'

If Kate really was an angel, come to take Jeff to heaven, then she made a very good one. She almost shone in the evening sunshine, which slanted across the porch—red-haired, with soft, honey-coloured eyes, which were unafraid of Sam's questions. Sam seemed to see it too, stepping towards her and laying his hand on her knee. Then he leaned forward, whispering into Kate's ear, and Ethan strained unsuccessfully to hear what he was saying.

'Yes, of course I will.' Kate crooked her little finger, hooking it around Sam's. 'There. That makes it a promise.'

Sam nodded, clearly satisfied, and ran into the house and straight up the stairs to his grandmother. Kate got to her feet.

'How's your arm?'

'Fine. Gives me a twinge now and then, but it's okay.'

She was smiling. She was wearing a short-sleeved top, which allowed Ethan to see that the bruises on her arm had faded now. More than that, there was a lightness about her. Maybe she'd been right in getting straight back to work. It seemed that the last three weeks had lifted the burden that had rested on her shoulders.

'I'm sorry about Sam ambushing you.'

'That's okay. He's working it out for himself.'

Ethan thought about asking Kate what Sam had said to her and decided against it. If Sam had wanted him to know, he wouldn't have made such a show of whispering in Kate's ear. It seemed that Sam had grasped the concept of having secrets now, and Ethan supposed he should respect that.

She leaned forward, the evening sunlight tangling in her hair. For a moment, Ethan couldn't move. 'Can I come in, then?'

'Oh. Yes, of course. Thanks for coming.'

He showed her through to the conservatory, and she walked across to Jeff's basket, kneeling down. It looked as if Jeff was just sleeping, and

Kate was stroking him gently, but Ethan knew that she was examining him.

'I think…' She looked up at him suddenly. 'Is Sam going now?'

'Yes, in a minute. As soon as my mother gets his things together. I think he's been waiting to see you.'

She pressed her lips together, in an unspoken understanding that this was hard. 'I think that if Sam has any goodbyes to say…'

'No, it's okay. I've been talking to him about this, and he's done what he wants to do.' Ethan indicated the drawing taped up by Jeff's basket. Sam had drawn himself, so that Jeff could show the picture to Jenna.

'That's nice.' Kate looked at the drawing and smiled, seeming to understand Sam's intentions.

'I'll go and see what he's doing.' Suddenly he wanted Sam away from here, so that he could keep what was left of his innocence of the realities of death for just a little longer. Ethan didn't want his son to see what he'd seen so often at the hospital.

'Okay. I'll stay here, with Jeff.'

Sam had gone, and Ethan no longer had to smile and pretend that everything was okay. He walked back into the conservatory and found

Kate where he'd left her, kneeling on the floor next to Jeff's basket.

'Would you like to sit with him a while?'

This wasn't what Ethan had expected. He'd already said his goodbyes to Jeff, privately and out of Sam's earshot, anticipating that Kate would arrive and gently suggest that it was time to put Jeff to sleep. It would be over in a moment.

Suddenly he *did* want to spend a little more time with his old friend. But a little more time was what everyone always wanted, wasn't it?

'Don't you have to go?'

She shook her head. 'No, there's nowhere I have to be. Would you like me to make you a cup of tea?'

He was taking advantage of her time and her good nature. But Ethan couldn't resist. 'Thanks. I'd really like that.'

He picked up the large floor cushion that Sam liked to sprawl on from the corner of the room and sat down on it next to Jeff's basket, his hand straying to Jeff's head. Kate watched him, then nodded quickly, as if everything was going exactly as she wanted it to and disappeared into the kitchen.

He could hear her clattering quietly around, opening and closing cupboards. The temptation to get up and show her where the mugs and teabags were drifted away. Ethan was exactly where he was supposed to be at that moment.

The kettle took its time to boil, and Kate took her time making the tea. She walked back into the conservatory, holding two mugs, and put them down on the table next to him, pulling one of the wicker chairs across to the other side of Jeff's basket.

'Which one's yours?' Ethan reached for the mugs and she shrugged, so he picked up one and tasted it. 'Ugh. Too sweet…'

She grinned at him. 'That's because I'm not sweet enough.'

Ethan would take issue with that. Kate's sweetness wasn't like sugar, liable to melt at the first drop of adversity. It was like steel, unbending but true. He wanted her here, now, not just for Jeff but for himself.

She leaned back in her seat, sipping her tea. Clearly she wasn't going anywhere for a few precious minutes.

It didn't always happen like this. Sometimes an animal was in pain, and sometimes Kate didn't have the opportunity to wait with an owner while it drifted away. But now wasn't one of those times, and they could let nature take its course, secure in the knowledge that the drugs in Kate's bag could be used if they were needed.

Ethan wasn't ready to say goodbye yet, but he was getting there. She could see the small stress lines around his eyes begin to relax as the light grew dimmer. Kate lit one of the fat candles lined up along the low windowsill and they talked quietly in the flickering light. Waiting.

Jeff's sleep became deeper and his breathing slowed, stopping for long moments and then starting again. Ethan must have known that the time was coming, and he leaned over, his lips just inches away from Jeff's head.

'Go to sleep now, boy. Everything's all right.'

CHAPTER FOUR

THE MOMENT THAT Ethan had dreaded became something peaceful that didn't feel as if something was tearing chunks out of his heart. Kate had waited a little while and then tucked Jeff's blanket over him, almost as if he really was just asleep.

This time Ethan made the tea, deciding at the last moment that as he wasn't driving he could have a glass of wine. Kate refused a half-glass for herself, and they sat on the steps which ran down from the open door of the conservatory onto the dark lawn.

'To Jeff.' She clinked her mug against his glass and Ethan smiled.

'Yeah, to Jeff.' He took a sip of the wine. 'Thanks for staying. I… I actually don't have the words to tell you how much I appreciate it.'

She nodded, staring straight ahead of her. 'You're welcome. We're not always lucky enough to be able to say goodbye to a friend like this but, when we can, it's something I want to try to make possible.'

'Well, thank you for making it possible this time. Can I ask you a question?' He'd tried to let go of the idea, but couldn't.

'Yes?' She turned to him, her eyes bright in the darkness. The thought that, if he reached for her, she might melt against him in the warmth of a summer evening's embrace almost made Ethan choke.

'What did Sam say to you?'

'Ah. I wondered when you'd get around to asking.'

'Is it a secret?' Ethan wasn't sure quite what he'd say if it was. He wouldn't blame Sam for wanting to share his secrets with Kate, but somehow it would seem like a rejection.

'No, it's not a secret. He said that I was to look after you.'

A tear pricked suddenly at the corner of Ethan's eye, and he rubbed his hand across his face, trying to cover the emotion. But it seemed that Kate wasn't fooled and she leaned towards him, bumping her shoulder gently against his arm.

'Growing up fast, is he?'

'Yeah. Very.'

'You said he was kind, and he is. That's a real credit to you.'

Ethan nodded. 'Yes he is. I'm not sure whether I taught him that, though, he seems to have come up with it all by himself.'

He heard Kate chuckle quietly beside him. 'I imagine that kindness is one of those things you get by example. You're worried about him?'

Ethan laughed. 'I'm *always* worried about him. That comes with the territory. Since Jenna died, I do the worrying for both of us.'

The words just slipped out. Maybe the darkness, and maybe the way that tonight had stripped away the boundaries. Or perhaps the way that Kate seemed to understand everything so well. Ethan tried to think of something to change the subject, and then he turned into her gaze.

She was wide-eyed and unflinching. When he talked about Jenna most people averted their gaze, but Kate didn't. 'I imagine that comes with the territory too. You must miss her very much.'

That wasn't an easy question to answer. Usually he would say, yes, he *did* miss Jenna, but tonight the simple response didn't seem enough.

'The first anniversary was hard. Sam and I… We're learning to move forward.' Ethan shrugged. 'Actually, he seems to have a momentum all of his own. I'm learning to keep up with him.'

Kate nodded. No questions. But, in the silence, Ethan felt that he could give whatever answer he wanted to.

'When Sam does something new, I miss not telling her about it.' Or just having *someone* to tell. Ethan wasn't sure which. But, since he'd promised himself he'd never let another woman down the way he had Jenna, he probably would never know.

'Jenna died very suddenly, and I'm not sure that she heard me when I told her I'd look after Sam...'

'I don't imagine she would have been in any doubt about that. It's obvious that Sam's your first priority.'

Ethan nodded. Here, now, it didn't seem so difficult to allow Kate in, even if it was just for a short time. If falling in love a second time would require a completely different skill set from any that he'd needed before, then perhaps Kate could teach him.

Ethan rejected the thought. They could be friends, without the complicating factor of his wanting to protect her all the time. Knowing that wasn't enough and that he should give all his energies to Sam.

'Time heals a lot of things.' He resorted to the familiar cliché and saw Kate nod.

It was getting darker, but Kate showed no

signs of wanting to leave. Ethan didn't want her to go. He wanted these moments of quiet peace to last.

'Sam's been talking about a new puppy.' It seemed suddenly quite natural that Ethan should share it with Kate.

'Yes? What do you think?'

'I think…it's a really good idea. And it'll be good for Sam.'

'A little bit soon for you, though?' Kate wasn't afraid to voice Ethan's one reservation.

'Yes. But if it's what Sam wants, then that's fine with me. I wondered if you could recommend anyone.' The small hope that she couldn't still tugged at his heart.

Kate nodded, staring silently out into the darkness for a moment, her lips pursed in thought. 'Yes, I do know a couple of people who have litters of pups which are ready for new homes. Were you thinking of any particular breed?'

'Not another Newfoundland. Jeff was always so beautifully tempered, and he was great with kids, but he was a bit big for Sam to take for walks. Something a bit smaller would suit him better.'

'Yes, I'm sure it would. Can I suggest an alternative to taking a puppy home right away?'

'If you're going to tell me to wait, then that's

not an option.' Ethan had already made that decision. Sam's wants and needs came first.

'I hear you. But one of our veterinary nurses is hand-rearing a litter. They're far too small to be rehomed just yet but Sam could choose one. You could visit every now and then, he'd see it grow, and then you could take the puppy when it's older.'

Ethan stared at her. He hadn't expected Kate to come up with a solution that would suit both him and Sam. 'That's… I think that Sam would really like that. What breed are they?'

'There's no pedigree certificate, but we know where they came from.' She grinned. 'They're definitely beagles. You can take my word on that.'

'Pretty good size for Sam, then.'

'I would think so, and generally speaking beagles are good with children. They need a lot of exercise, though, and you can't leave a beagle pup on its own all day while you're at work.'

'That wouldn't be a problem. My parents live in one of the villages about twenty minutes away from here. They look after Sam during the holidays and after school, and my dad's already said if Sam wants a puppy they'd take care of it while I'm at work. He's almost as keen on the idea as Sam is.'

Ethan made his decision, finding that it wasn't as difficult as he'd thought it would be.

'Would it be okay if we came to have a look at them?'

'Yes, of course. Give me a ring, whenever you're ready.' She shot him a mischievous grin. 'If one of the puppies chooses you, then Sam can visit any time he likes.'

'Thank you. That's very kind.' Ethan wanted to hug her, but that wouldn't be quite fair. She'd hug him back, thinking he needed comfort, but that wasn't his motive. He just wanted to feel her, soft in his arms.

'It's my pleasure.'

There were no words for this. Sitting here with Kate, the light from the house casting warm shadows around them. If he could just make tonight something which stood by itself, which had no yesterday to sour it and no tomorrow to make it impossible, then he would have kissed her.

'I'm going to take Jeff now.' Her gentle words interrupted the dream of what Ethan knew couldn't happen. 'You can pop in over the next couple of days and see our receptionist to make arrangements.'

If he'd thought about it, Ethan would have known all along that Kate would take Jeff. He just hadn't been able to face it. Now he could.

He tipped the contents of his glass into the flower bed next to the steps.

'I'll come with you.'

She hesitated, then shook her head firmly. 'No, that's okay. I'd appreciate it if you could give me a hand getting him into my car, but I'll be fine once I get to the surgery.'

Kate might feel okay about this, but he didn't. It was one thing to rationalise about lightning not striking twice, but quite another thing to leave her to negotiate the darkness outside the surgery.

'I'd like to just…see Jeff off. And, now I've thrown away three quarters of a glass of a very nice Chablis, it's the least you can do to let me tag along. I might go to my parents and spend the night there, so I'm around for Sam when he wakes up.'

'Okay. That sounds like a good idea.'

Ethan supressed a smile, wondering if he might add that he'd follow her home and see her inside. But there was an obvious flaw in the assertion that her place was on his way to his parents' house, which was that he didn't know where Kate lived. Maybe he'd work his way round to suggesting that later.

Ethan seemed to want the company and Kate had to admit that she was very glad he was there. They'd carried Jeff into the surgery together, and Ethan hadn't left her side until she was safely back in her car. Then he'd bent down, tapping on the window.

'Which way are you going?'

'I live in Eadleigh. On the edge of the village.'

His face broke into a broad grin. 'It's on my way. I'll follow you and see you inside.'

The last time she'd negotiated the dark shadows which crowded in on her front path at night, she'd forced herself to walk and not run, but had still arrived inside the house breathless and pushing away the panic. Kate would certainly appreciate him being there, but she didn't want to admit it.

He turned suddenly, not waiting for her answer, and got into his car.

She parked in the lane outside her cottage, dimly aware that the lights of his car, which had shone reassuringly behind her all the way from the surgery, had just been extinguished. She looked in the rear-view mirror and saw him swing out of the driver's seat.

Okay. So he was a gentleman. The closeness that had tingled in the air between them this evening somehow made this a more obvious move than it otherwise might have been. Kate got out of her car, marching towards him.

'I'd ask you in but the place is a terrible mess.

End of the week, you know? I do my housework on a Saturday…' She pressed her lips together. She was protesting too much and, if Ethan couldn't see the lie on her face in the darkness, he might well hear it in her voice.

He shrugged. 'Yeah, I know.'

'Well, goodnight, Ethan. I'm so sorry you lost Jeff this evening.'

He nodded. 'I think we both did our best for him and that means a lot. Thank you.'

Kate swallowed the impulse to hug him, and turned, hurrying up the front path. As she fumbled for her keys in her handbag, she saw Ethan leaning against his car, watching her inside, and breathed a word of thanks that she knew he couldn't hear.

Waving to him, she closed the front door, shooting the bolt on the new deadlock. Everything was quiet, undisturbed. Just the way she'd left it this morning. The back door was locked and the windows were secure.

She walked into the sitting room, slumping into a chair. The place was clean and rather relentlessly tidy, to the point that it looked a little starker than usual. During the hours when she wasn't either at work or trying to sleep she'd been keeping herself busy, finding that physical effort gave her some relief from the clamour of her thoughts.

She *could* have asked him in—offered him a cup of tea, given him the opportunity to talk a little more if he'd wanted to. But somehow, asking anyone into her home, her sanctuary, was a little more than she was able to do at the moment. Here she was safe.

Safe from the feeling that it would feel good just to curl up with Ethan and go to sleep, undisturbed by the nightmares. He'd taken on the role of hero in her imagination and this couldn't go on. His eyes were just eyes and they didn't need any adjectives to describe them.

She looked at her watch, stifling a yawn. She had an early call tomorrow and she hadn't had a great deal of sleep last night. Hopefully tonight would be different.

CHAPTER FIVE

JOY. THE EMOTION came before Kate had the opportunity to temper it with reason. Her phone caught her unawares and when she saw Ethan's name on the caller display there was one moment of pure, heart-stopping joy.

'Hi, Ethan. How are things?' Her voice sounded strangely breathless and Kate looked around at the crowded waiting room full of patients for her evening surgery to see if anyone had noticed.

'Good, thanks. Are you okay?'

'Yes. I'm good.'

That got the denial over and done with. The last few days couldn't have been easy for Ethan, and they hadn't been easy for Kate either. But she was managing, and she couldn't imagine that Ethan was doing any differently.

'I was wondering if it would be okay for me and Sam to see the puppies you were talking about. Um, hold on a minute...'

Kate grinned. The shrill voice in the background told her that Sam was obviously getting excited at the prospect.

'Sorry about that. Sam! Holding your breath isn't going to make any difference.'

People were starting to look. Kate hurried into her empty surgery to hide the stupid grin on her face. 'When do you want to come and see them?'

'Would the weekend be convenient for you?'

Kate was taking the puppies this weekend. She dismissed the feeling that it would be better to see Ethan again on neutral ground. She should look at it as seeing Sam. Letting *him* into her home, her safe place, was a great deal easier to contemplate.

'The weekend would be fine. Sue, the nurse who's looking after them, is going away, and I'm going to be taking them. How about Friday evening? I'm finishing work early.' From the sounds in the background, the sooner the better for Ethan. He obviously had a very excited child on his hands.

'Friday would be great.'

'That's good. Come to my place around seven. Do you remember where I live?'

'Yes. I remember.'

'Okay...' An awkward silence reminded Kate that really the only connection she had with

Ethan was a professional one, even though it felt so very personal. 'I'll see you then. I'm in the middle of a surgery. I've got to run.'

'Of course. Thanks, I'll see you tomorrow.' The line abruptly cut out. Maybe the excitement was just too much for Sam and Ethan had to go and calm him down. Or maybe, that was really all they had to say to each other.

Settling the puppies into their home for the weekend had taken a while. Kate looked around the cottage and decided against vacuuming in favour of changing out of her work clothes. The top that she picked from the wardrobe was one that she rarely wore, but particularly liked.

'Stupid little…' Her fingers fumbled with the tiny mother-of-pearl buttons. Ethan wasn't going to notice, and Sam almost certainly wouldn't. Maybe the pups would like it, but if they gnawed at the fine cotton she'd be sorry.

Pulling the scrunchie out, she brushed her hair. That was going to have to do. Any more and it might give the impression that she'd dressed up, and dressing up to spend Friday evening at home wasn't really her style any more.

There was a time when it had been. After the first mugging, she'd returned home from the hospital and locked herself in her flat. Locking out the hurt and the fear. Telling herself that she had to cope alone, because no one else would help her.

And she'd stayed there for six months, immobilised at first and struggling to get out to the hospital for her outpatient appointments. Her body had healed, but her heart hadn't, and she'd found herself alone, hardly ever going out and never letting anyone in.

As soon as she'd been able to, she'd dressed up on a Friday evening, marking the end of the week in the same way that ordinary people did, despite the fact that her weekends were pretty much the same as her weekdays. She'd cooked a nice meal and settled down to watch a film on the TV.

That wasn't her any more. She'd given in to the fear after she'd been mugged the first time, but this time it would be different. She would go out and invite people over just like any other normal human being. And Kate had to admit that she was looking forward to seeing Ethan, even if it meant letting him and his son into her home.

The sound of a car in the lane outside reached her. Hers was the last cottage in the row and it was either Ethan or someone who'd taken a wrong turn and got lost. Kate approached the window, standing back from the net curtains so that its occupants couldn't see her. Ethan's dark-blue SUV was manoeuvring into a parking space.

She paced up and down the hallway impatiently. How long did it take to get one child out of a car and up the front path? Kate was just considering peeping through the letter box to see what was going on when the doorbell rang.

'Hold the flowers, Sam.' Ethan retrieved the small bunch of flowers from the footwell of his car and put them on the back seat next to Sam.

'Dad!' Sam clearly wasn't in the mood for flowers. He was in the mood for puppies and viewed anything else as an obstacle.

The choosing and buying of flowers and their careful arrangement into the kind of posy that a child might give had been a calculated time waster, intended to fill the hour between picking up Sam from his parents' and arriving at Kate's house. But, even though the urge to give them to Kate himself had grown during the course of the exercise, it was impossible.

'Come on, Sam. Kate's helping us, and this is our way of saying thank you to her.'

'But she's not my girlfriend!' Sam protested.

'She doesn't have to be your girlfriend for us to give her flowers. It's a way of saying thank you. Like when we give Grandma flowers.'

'Is she going to kiss me?' When Sam presented Ethan's mother with flowers, there was always a protracted phase of hugging and kissing before the blooms were whisked off to the kitchen to be arranged.

'I wouldn't think so. Just give her the flowers and then she'll show you the puppies.'

'Oh.' Sam thought about it for a moment and then picked up the posy. 'Okay.'

Ethan breathed a sigh of relief and climbed out of the car, opening the back door to release Sam from his car seat. His son scarpered up the front path, almost dropping the flowers as he stretched for the doorbell. Ethan lifted him up so he could reach, putting him back down on his feet before Sam could jab his finger on the bell a second time.

Sam shuffled impatiently on the doorstep, looking as if he was about to kick the front door in an attempt to gain entry. Ethan laid his hand on his son's shoulder and the door opened. And then he forgot that he'd told himself that this visit was all about Sam, as his whole world suddenly upended.

Kate was wearing a thin, white cotton top with a green patterned border at the neck. It was practical and pretty, the kind of thing lots of women wore in the summer, but Kate made everything she wore seem special. Her hair curled around her shoulders, free of the pins and elastic bands that restrained it while she was at work. In the week since he'd seen her last, she seemed to have grown softer and prettier. Or maybe it was just that his memory wasn't up to recreating her perfectly.

Sam stepped forward, thrusting the flowers at her. 'From Dad.'

Thanks, mate. Kate flushed a little, the delicate red of her cheeks making Ethan wish for a moment that the arrangement of white roses and freesias *were* from him. She took the posy, reading the tag which dangled from the raffia binding.

'It says here they're from you, Sam. Did you write that?'

'Yes. They're from me.' Sam seemed to think nothing of the abrupt *volte face*. 'Where are the puppies?'

'Come with me. They're through here.' Kate held out her hand and Sam took it, glancing back at Ethan as he followed them inside, closing the front door behind him.

She led the way through a small kitchen, neat and gleaming, the astringent smell of cleaning fluid still in the air despite the open window. An open door at the far end was barred by a child gate, and beyond that was a bright, airy room, the walls painted cream and the floor covered with newspaper and dog toys. In the corner was a high-sided wooden box.

Kate bent down to Sam. 'We have to be very quiet and gentle with them. They're only tiny and we don't want to frighten them.'

Sam nodded, leaning towards Kate to whisper to her. 'Can we go inside?'

'Yes, of course we can.' She swung open the child gate and led Sam into the room.

Ethan tried to ignore the four tiny forms curled up inside the box and lingered by the doorway, keeping his gaze on his son. Sam's eyes were as wide as saucers, and he was tiptoeing up to the box, trying very hard to be quiet.

'What do you think, Sam?' Kate bent down next to him, one hand resting lightly on his back. Just the right amount of reassurance, yet still allowing Sam the space to explore this new experience.

'They're little…' Sam was obviously considering the practicalities of taking one of the tiny creatures for a walk and playing ball with it.

'Yes, they're very small now, but they're still growing. In a few weeks' time they'll be this big.' She held her hands out.

'That's the right size.'

'Yes, I think so too. Would you like to touch one of them?'

Sam twisted round, looking questioningly at

Ethan, and he nodded. 'Yes, that's all right. Gently, so you don't hurt them.'

Sam reached into the box, his fingertips touching the puppy closest to him. It roused from its sleep and gave a little whelping bark, and Sam snatched his hand away.

'It's all right. He's just saying hello to you.' Kate dangled her hand inside the box and the puppy responded, licking her fingers. Sam caught his breath, holding his hand out, and Kate moved her fingers next to his so that the puppy moved across to lick Sam's hand.

'Dad, look, he's licking me.' Sam's face was shining with the kind of wonder that only a child had access to on a day-to-day basis.

'Yes, that's okay. Your dad can see.'

Kate was giving him a little space, allowing him to stand back, but suddenly Ethan didn't want to. If Jeff had been here, he probably would have ambled up to the puppies and tried to get into the box with them.

Ethan stepped forward, catching the scent of flowers as he bent down next to Kate—bright and clean, with an undertone of something sensual, like a summer's afternoon spent lying on a blanket in the middle of a meadow. And then she was gone, leaving him to talk to Sam and play with the puppies with him.

* * *

Kate had given the puppies a bowl of food so that Sam could watch them eat, then ushered Ethan and him out onto the back garden, installing Sam in a child's garden chair next to the door which led from the utility room onto the patio.

Ethan's tall frame made the table and two chairs that sat on the paved area seem even smaller. He sat down, looking at the riot of spring colour that stretched twenty yards from the back of the cottage and spilled around each of its sides. Kate was pleased with the way her garden was coming along this year.

'You're a gardener, then.' Ethan laughed when she shrugged. 'It takes a lot of hard work to make a garden look this random and natural.'

He'd noticed. Kate suppressed a smile and set about arranging the teacups on the table. 'This is the second summer I've been here. I did a lot of planting last year, and I'm beginning to enjoy the results.'

'It's nice here. Quiet.'

That was one of the things that had attracted Kate to this place, away from the hustle of London. Away from the memories and the fears. But now it brought new fears. She realised that she hadn't sat out here in her garden for a few weeks, contenting herself with viewing it from behind the locked windows of the kitchen.

'We don't get a lot of through traffic.'

He nodded, his gaze following the trajectory of the lane that passed in front of her cottage and continued straight for another hundred yards. It then curled in an arc and stopped short.

'Where does the lane lead?'

Kate smiled. It wasn't the first time someone had asked the question. 'This cottage used to be the second-to-last in the lane. There was another one further along, but I'm told it burned down about fifty years ago. You can still see the foundations if you walk down there.'

'You have a great view.' He nodded towards Summer Hill rising in the distance, and Kate remembered that he'd said it was his favourite place. 'I miss living in the countryside. My parents have a couple of acres out by Hambleton and I was brought up there.'

'I imagine living in the town's more convenient. With Sam...'

He shrugged. 'It has its pros and cons. It's further away from a community where everyone knows everyone else.'

'Yes, I've been learning all about that. I'm still the new girl here, but there's always something going on. I've managed to get on one of the teams for quiz night at the pub.'

Ethan chuckled. 'You're well on your way to becoming a local, then. I hope you take it seriously.'

'Very seriously. My grasp of anatomy came in useful last week.'

'What made you move up here?' He turned suddenly, as if this was a question that was more than just idle talk filling in the time while Sam stared at the puppies.

'I just wanted to make a new start. Have my own garden and a bit of fresh air. If this place was in London I wouldn't be able to even think about affording it.'

His gaze held hers for a moment, as if he knew that there was more to it than that. His dark-blue eyes were almost mesmerising, sucking her in and demanding the truth. And then he looked away.

'I think he's found a new friend.' One of the puppies had finished eating and come to the doorway, pressing itself against the piece of wood that Kate had wedged across the threshold to stop the puppies from escaping.

She craned round to look at Sam, who was stroking the puppy and talking to it quietly. 'He doesn't need to make a decision yet.'

'I think I've made mine.' Ethan caught his son's attention. 'Sam, would you like it if we took one of these puppies home when it's a bit bigger?'

'Can we have them all?'

'I think one's enough.'

'Two?' Sam was obviously open to a bit of bargaining.

Kate giggled. 'But where are you going to get the time to play with two of them?'

Sam thought about it for a moment and nodded sagely. 'All right. Just one.'

Ethan's blue eyes were all she could see as he looked back at her. 'How old are they—six weeks?'

'Five and a half. As I said, they've no pedigree certificates, but they all come with a clean bill of health, and Sue's done a great job with socialising them. We're hoping to find homes for them to go to at eight weeks, but I can take the one you choose after that. Until you're ready.'

'Two and a half weeks will be fine.' Ethan nodded towards Sam, who had gone back to stroking the puppy. 'That's a very long time when you're five.'

'And when you're a bit older than five?' Kate didn't want to push Ethan.

'It's quite long enough to deal with a five-year-old who can't wait.' Ethan turned to Sam, catching his attention again. 'Is that the one, Sam?'

Sam turned his shining face up to him and nodded.

'You're sure?'

'Yes, Dad.'

Ethan chuckled. 'Good choice. We'd like to take that one, please, Kate.'

Suddenly her cottage became a home again. One where she might just think about opening the windows and allowing the perfumed breeze in, instead of locking it up like a fortress.

'He's yours.'

'Thank you. How much…?' Ethan reached into his jacket for his wallet.

'It'll cost you a good home and a lot of love. Nothing more.'

He nodded. 'Fair enough. Pick a charity, then.'

Kate thought about telling him no, but he obviously wanted to give something. 'The local mountain rescue? I'm a member. I help with the dog training exercises and give them their health checks. They're based over in Highbridge'

'I know it. That would be a pleasure.'

'Thank you.' Kate rose from her chair, trying to shake off the feeling that she wanted to reach across the table and touch Ethan's hand. When she picked up the puppy, Sam jumped to his feet, following her back to his father's side.

She caught a brief hint of Ethan's scent as

she bent to deliver the puppy into his arms. Not enough to savour properly, but more than enough to want more. Kate straightened, turning to Sam.

'I'll let you and your Dad hold him for a while. So he can get to know you.'

'Yessss!' Sam looked as if he was about to burst from excitement, responding to Ethan's, 'What do you say?' with a hurried 'Thank you.'

Kate left them to it. Ethan's gentle hands and smouldering eyes. A little boy and his first puppy. Watching all that was more than she could bear, when there was no chance that she could have any of it. And she'd noticed a few weeds amongst the flowers which suddenly needed her urgent attention.

CHAPTER SIX

ETHAN STARED AT his phone. His head told him that there was nothing wrong with the text. But his gut told him that everything was wrong with it.

Car broken down, on way back from Hallowes Common. Waiting for pick-up. Will be about half an hour late tonight, but will call when I am on my way. Sorry.

It all seemed perfectly straightforward. Kate was going to examine all the puppies at the surgery this evening, and she'd told Ethan that he could bring Sam over if he wanted. She was going to be half an hour late, that was all.

But he knew Kate better than that. Talking allowed more give and take than texting, and it conveyed more warmth. If Kate's first instinct was to text, then he'd be willing to bet that there was something wrong. He could feel a prickling sensation crawling along the back of his neck.

He was making something out of nothing. He was about to leave work, and it would take twenty minutes to get from the hospital to his parents' house, to pick up Sam. He'd stay there, until Kate phoned to say that she was ready.

Or… Hallowes Common was twenty minutes in the other direction.

Kate was breathing so fast that her head was swimming. The hollow feeling in her chest felt as if it was about to swallow her. She put the paper bag over her mouth again, watching it inflate and deflate.

This wasn't happening. Okay, so it *was* happening, but she could deal with it. Her car had broken down, that was all. People's cars broke down all the time.

Squinting through her tears, she could see a car coming, appearing and disappearing as it negotiated the curves in the road ahead. Perhaps she should hide her keys. The chasm in her chest suddenly opened further and she let out a little cry of frustration at her own inability to cope.

Fixing her gaze on the steering wheel, she breathed into the bag. One… Two… Concentrate… She felt her heartbeat slow a little. And then the car that she'd seen in the distance rounded the corner.

Ethan. No. Not here. Not now.

She threw the paper bag into the footwell, trying to slow her breathing. Not daring to look him in the face as he walked towards her, she fixed her gaze on his left shoulder.

He reached the driver's door, squatting down next to it. He must have come straight from work. She hadn't seen Ethan in a white shirt and tie before. Even though the tie had been loosened and the shirt was open at the neck, he looked quite devastatingly reliable.

The 'R' word again. *Don't even think it. Don't think the 'H' word, either.* It was difficult not to, because she didn't actually need to look at him to know he was handsome, she remembered all too well what he looked like.

Slowly, he raised his arm, circling his hand in an indication that she should put the window down. Kate complied with the instruction in a haze of misery.

'Hey, there.' He reached in, tipping her face gently towards him. 'Car's broken down, eh?'

'Yes.' Maybe he hadn't noticed the state she'd got herself into.

'Okay.' He lifted the tab on the inside of the door, and she heard the central locking disengage. Then he opened the door, bending down again next to her.

'Here.' He managed to retrieve the paper bag from the footwell without touching her. 'Just breathe.'

She couldn't resist his quiet, authoritative tone. It felt that, if she just did what Ethan said, everything would be all right.

'Better?'

She nodded wordlessly.

'All right. Keep going.'

She started to count again in her head, and then realised she was going too fast. Ethan was counting slower. When she followed his lead, the panic that was reverberating in her chest began to recede a little.

It seemed like an age but finally he stopped counting and her own rhythm took over. She felt surer now and stronger. She crumpled the paper bag in her lap, and Ethan nodded.

'Give me your keys. I'll go and get your bag from the back of your car and we'll go and sit in mine. Then we'll phone and find out where the tow truck is.'

He knew exactly what to do. Kate handed him her keys, feeling the car rock slightly as he opened the boot. Then the sound of him unlocking the boot safe. He reappeared, carrying her veterinary bag in one hand and the smaller drugs bag in the other.

'Are you going to look at the engine?' That was what any self-respecting hero would do. He'd look under the bonnet and tell her to try the ignition. The engine would then choke reluctantly back to life.

Ethan raised one eyebrow. 'No. I'm a doctor, not a car mechanic. We'll wait for the tow truck.'

'Oh. Good.' The thought that Ethan had at least one chink in his armour was oddly reassuring. Kate got out of the car and followed him over to his, watching as he stowed her bags under the back seat and opened the passenger door for her.

'Are you on any medication?' When Kate got into the car, he bent down beside her again.

'No!'

He grinned suddenly. 'Fair enough. Have you changed the oil in your car recently?'

'So you *are* a mechanic, then.'

'No. I just thought you might like that line of questioning a little better. How quickly did you stop?'

'Slowly. I didn't need the brakes, but as far as I know they're okay as well.'

'Good to know. Look at my finger.' He held one finger up, moving it from side to side.

He could be forgiven for thinking she'd hit something, or bumped her head, after all the fuss she'd made. 'The engine just cut out and the car stopped. It's an old car and I've been thinking I should get a new one. I just...panicked a bit. Stupid.' She was feeling better now. Stronger. As if a smile wasn't totally out of the question.

'All right. Have you got the number of the garage? I'll give them a call and see where they are.'

A little of the colour had returned to her cheeks. Ethan swallowed the temptation to ask Kate why on earth she hadn't called and asked him to pick her up, and concentrated on the practicalities. Getting her out of the car and making sure she was all right.

The tow truck was out on another call, and he'd agreed that they'd leave the car and drop the keys in at the garage. Kate sat silently as he drove back into town and delivered her car keys to the mechanic.

'I'll take you home.' He got back into the driver's seat and started the engine.

'No—thank you, but I have to go to the surgery. And you need to pick up Sam. He'll be wanting to see his puppy.'

Her reaction was entirely expected. Ethan had

his answer ready. 'He can see it another time. I called my parents to let them know, when I went to talk to the mechanic.'

'But he'll be disappointed.'

'Yes, he will. But it's not the end of the world, and he knows that he'll see the puppy soon. It's more important that you go home.'

'I can't, I have things to do. I just had a bit of a moment. It was stupid and I'm okay now.'

Ethan sighed. He'd expected that Kate would object, and she hadn't disappointed him. A garage forecourt probably wasn't the best place to do this, but at least the car afforded them some privacy.

'Look, I don't want to interfere—'

'Then don't.' She flashed a warning glare in his direction.

'All right, then, I *do* want to interfere. You're very clearly trying to pretend that nothing's wrong, and most of the time when you're with people, that's working pretty well. But for some of the time, probably when you're alone, I think you're suffering from symptoms of stress. Panic attacks...nightmares, maybe.'

The look in her eyes told him that his gamble had just paid off and that he was right. 'Some of the time isn't so bad, is it?'

'It's not so good, either. Did the police put you in touch with a victim support officer?'

'I'm *not* a victim!' The words were said with such vehemence that Ethan knew he'd touched a nerve. He pushed a little more.

'You're not afraid of allowing me a bit of time to process things, Kate. Why are you so afraid of doing the same for yourself? You'll heal if you just let yourself.'

That was it. She was suddenly white-faced and trembling. It was the healing, not the attack itself, that had the power to frighten her. And from what he knew of her, Kate didn't frighten easily.

'What happened—the last time you were attacked?'

'Does it matter?'

'Yes, I'm pretty sure that it does. Can you tell me?'

She stared at him, pressing her lips together as if she were trying to stop the words coming from her mouth.

'Kate, you're a strong woman. That's why I'm asking you to tell me.'

One tear escaped her eye and ran down her cheek. 'There were two of them. They grabbed me and took my bag. Searched me for jewellery.'

Ethan shivered. That small detail seemed like the worst thing—unable to escape and being searched, none too gently he imagined. 'And then?'

'I was at the top of the steps which led down to the underground—it happened in London.'

Ethan nodded her on, almost afraid to hear what came next.

'They pushed me down the steps. I fell all the way.'

'And you were hurt badly?' The last time he'd asked that question she'd refused to answer. Ethan suspected she'd been hurt *very* badly, both physically and mentally.

'It wasn't as bad as it might have been. Concussion and a fractured ankle. Broken shoulder.' She tried to smile and Ethan felt his hand move across the seat towards her. Her injuries were bad enough that they would have left Kate immobile for a while. They would have taken away her only coping mechanisms...her independence and her ability to work.

'What then?' Something told him that there was more.

'I...' She heaved a sigh, but her gaze didn't leave his face. 'When I couldn't get out, because of my injuries, it wasn't so bad. But when I started to get back on my feet physically, the panic attacks began. I couldn't sleep and I'd constantly be checking the locks on the doors. I didn't go out of my flat for six months.'

If Ethan had ever doubted that she had the courage to tell him everything, now he didn't.

The little tilt of her head, the defiance in her eyes, was unmistakeable.

'Were you alone? When you were attacked?'

She shook her head. 'No, I was... I was with a man. Someone I was going out with.'

'What happened to him?' Ethan wondered whether guilt over what had happened to her companion played a part in this.

'He ran away. He felt pretty bad about it afterwards, I suppose, but I only saw him once after that.'

It wasn't guilt, then, it was betrayal. Ethan took a breath.

'Kate, you know what's happening here, don't you.'

'Yes, I know. I lost everything—my job, my boyfriend. I nearly lost my flat because I couldn't keep the payments on the mortgage up. Then I made a new start and I thought that it was all behind me. Now I'm afraid it's going to happen again.' Her voice was expressionless, as if adding the emotion into the words was a little too much for her to bear.

'Then you'll know what you need to do.'

'I need to just stop it. By myself, the way I did last time.'

'No, you need to get some help.' Ethan could see now why that would be difficult for her. The one person who had been supposed to help her the last time hadn't just run away, he hadn't come back afterwards.

'My boss mustn't know. You can't tell anyone…' Alarm flashed in her eyes, and a sudden shard of warmth dispersed the chill that had settled over Ethan. She'd trusted him enough to tell him.

'You're in my car. I'll take that to mean that doctor-patient privilege applies.'

'You're not *my* doctor.'

Her sudden smile ripped away the last of his defences. Ethan had been trying to approach this professionally, as if she was a patient who could be cared *for*, but not *about*. Getting involved wasn't something he did any more, and he'd almost forgotten how that went.

'I'm *a* doctor. That probably covers it.' He attempted a grin, and she nodded.

'Okay then, doctor. What's your solution?'

He struggled momentarily with the urge to take her in his arms. To tell her that it was all going to be all right and that he'd stay with her through the darkest of nights. Kate didn't need reassurance, though, she needed action.

'I have a friend. She works at the hospital. I've referred people who are traumatised by surgery to her before and she's excellent at what she does. I can introduce you to her and she'll see you out of hours. The only way that anyone else will ever know about this is if you choose to tell them.'

'She must be expensive.' At least Kate was thinking about it. She hadn't turned the idea down out of hand.

'I think it would be an excellent investment to see her privately for a few sessions, if she can see you straight away.' Ethan wondered if Kate could afford it, and whether he could get away with speaking to Dr Usha Patel privately and paying for her sessions himself.

Kate shook her head suddenly. 'I don't want to jump the queue. There must be other people who need her much more than I do.'

Ethan sighed. 'That's Usha's problem. Leave her to sort her diary out for herself. If she can't do it, she'll say.'

The internal struggle—that need to talk that Kate was constantly pushing away—was written all over her face. Finally she made the right decision.

'You're right. I'll call her.'

When she got around to it, no doubt. Which might well be never. Ethan nodded, picking up his phone and consulting his contacts list. Kate almost jumped out of her seat.

'What are you doing? It's six o'clock.'

'Yes, that's fine. She often works in the evening. And she owes me a favour.' He dialled

Usha's number, hoping that she wasn't with a client.

He heard Usha's voice on the line and grinned. Kate was fidgeting in her seat. He explained quickly that a friend was experiencing some problems and it would be great if she could spare some time to talk with her.

'I'm sorry to hear that. Yes, I have some free time, I can fit her in.'

'Thanks, Usha.' He glanced at Kate. 'She says she can fit you in.'

'Wait…' Usha's voice held a trace of firmness in her tone. 'She's there? Are you railroading her into this, Ethan? Let me speak with her.'

He hadn't anticipated that it would be Usha who threw a spoke in the wheel of his plan. But Ethan had to admit that she was right.

'Um…right. Okay.' He handed the phone to Kate. 'She'd like to speak with you. I'll…go and get some coffee.' He could see a café across the road, and it was the only excuse he could think of to get out of the car and give Kate some privacy. He opened the door, hearing her tremulous, 'Hello?' behind him.

He spent five minutes hanging around in the window of the café, nursing a cup of coffee that would have been fresh brewed an hour ago. Finally he saw Kate take the phone from her ear.

Ethan got into the car and, at a loss for anything more to say, he proffered his polystyrene cup to her. She took it wordlessly, taking a sip from it.

'Ew! What are you trying to do, poison me? I suppose that's one way of making me feel no pain.' She wrinkled her nose, putting the cup back into his hand.

The ice broke. Ethan grinned, tipping the contents of the cup out of the window and stowing it in the glove compartment, alongside a couple of empty cartons of Sam's favourite juice. 'Have you sorted things out with Usha?'

'It's all fixed. I'm going to see her tomorrow, after work.' Kate was obviously a lot happier about the idea now, and it occurred to Ethan that it was Usha who had put her mind at rest, not him.

'Good. I…um… I hope you didn't think I was railroading you.' He grinned stupidly. 'Actually, you'd be quite right if you did think that.'

Kate raised her eyebrows. 'Yes, I thought you were railroading me. It was what I needed, thank you.'

'It's my pleasure.' Ethan started the engine, and then realised he really should ask Kate where they were going next. 'Where to?'

'If you wouldn't mind giving me a lift to the surgery, I really do just need to pop in.'

'And then home?'

'Yes, thank you. Then home.'

Ethan nodded. It was time for him to back off and leave Usha and Kate to sort things out now. He'd won a victory, but somehow it had a bitter aftertaste.

CHAPTER SEVEN

USHA WAS NICE, dressed in soft shades of grey and purple, with dangly earrings and a down-to-earth attitude. She'd listened to what Kate had to say, nodding her on as if none of this was anything to be ashamed of.

Then, five minutes before the end of the session, she'd issued Kate a challenge. Maybe this therapy thing wasn't as easy as she'd thought. But Usha had smiled and shrugged, adding a proviso. 'Give it a try.'

'I'll do it.' If Usha thought that she couldn't, then Kate would prove her wrong.

'We'll make another appointment for early next week, then.' Usha smiled serenely, and Kate left the comfortable consulting room wondering what on earth she'd let herself in for.

Or what Ethan had let her in for. He knew Usha, and he must also know that this wasn't going to be easy. But he must think that she could do it.

The one thing she hadn't shared was the struggle to put Ethan into context and think of him as if he were just any other friend. She'd deal with that one on her own. It was far too embarrassing to talk to Usha about it. A little common sense would have to do.

And common sense told her that Ethan would lose some of his super-human powers if she concentrated on the Ethan who lived in the real world and not her imagination. Talking to him, instead of wishing he'd phone, would be a good idea. As she waited for the bus home, she dialled his number.

'Hello, Kate.' His tone was studiedly neutral, obviously waiting to see whether she'd kept the appointment she had with Usha before he said anything.

'Hi. I was thinking, since Sam didn't get to see the puppies yesterday, he might like to come to the working dog show we're holding at the weekend. It's not a very big one, just a local thing, but that could be nicer for him as he'll get to meet the dogs and their owners.'

There was a pause. Clearly he wasn't going to ask. 'That could be really nice. He'll be able to see what dogs can do when they're trained.'

'Well, it's on Saturday afternoon. In a little village called Hambleton. Do you know it?'

'Yes, I know it well. It's where my parents'

house is, remember? And it's pronounced "Hampton".'

'Really? Is that a concerted effort to confuse anyone who doesn't come from around here?'

'Yes, we do our best. Where is it, in the church hall?'

'Yes, that's right. Spelled St Thomas's, and you can pronounce it however you like.'

She heard Ethan chuckle quietly. 'What time?'

'Two o'clock. I'll be there from one-thirty onwards with the mountain rescue team.'

'Right. Should be interesting. Thanks for letting me know about it.'

'Great. See you then, perhaps.'

Silence crackled down the line. Kate couldn't help smiling, because she knew what Ethan wanted to ask, and this time she had an answer that didn't make her feel as if she wanted to disappear.

'For goodness' sake... Okay, you win. How did this evening go?' There was a note of exasperated humour in his tone.

'It went well, thank you. Usha's given me some homework.'

'What was that, then—phoning me up and giving me a hard time?'

'No, that might be next week's assignment, though.' It was a dream diary. Kate didn't feel quite comfortable about telling him that, because her nightmares were often the dreams where she was helpless and Ethan wasn't there to save her.

She heard him chuckle quietly. 'All right. I'm not going to ask, that's between you and Usha. As long as you feel it's been positive.'

'Yes, I do. Thanks for putting me in touch with her.'

'No problem. I'm going to go now, before you do my nervous system any more damage. Oh, hang on a minute.' She could hear Sam's voice in the background, and smiled. 'Sam says hello.'

'Tell him hello back. I'll see him on Saturday, if you're able to come.'

'We'll be there.'

Ethan joined the small crowd that had gathered outside the church, and found that its main topic of conversation consisted of whether it was one minute to two or one minute past. Events such as these were usually attended by the stalwarts of the surrounding villages, most of whom were retired. They arrived on time, all knew each other and departed after half an hour, which was when the younger families would start to arrive.

'Hello, Ethan.' He'd known Mrs Sweetman since he was a child, and had thought her very old then. 'You're very early, dear.'

'Yes, I...' Couldn't wait to see Kate? If he were to voice that, then it would be old news by sundown. 'I happened to be passing.'

'With Sam, I see.' Mrs Sweetman smiled down at his son. 'How you've grown, dear.'

'Hello. I'm five now.' Sam responded with the same courtesy towards the elders of the village that Ethan had been taught.

'Are you, now? Doesn't time fly? I wonder when they're going to open the doors?'

'You can sync your phone, Mrs Sweetman. Then you'll know the right time.'

A little burst of pride made Ethan smile. He'd shown Sam how he synched the time display on his phone last week and his son had clearly been listening far more closely than it had appeared at the time.

'My telephone?' Mrs Sweetman was clearly thinking of an apparatus connected to the wall by a wire. 'That sounds rather clever.'

'Dad will show you. He showed me on his phone.' Sam seemed eager to help and Ethan breathed a small sigh of relief as the doors of the church hall opened. Offering Mrs Sweetman his arm, he walked slowly inside.

Kate was nowhere to be seen. Display boards with photographs were laid out on one side of the hall and a tea table on the other. The crowd migrated as one to the tea table.

'Where are the dogs, Dad?' Sam was looking a little disappointed.

'They'll be outside. We'll go and see them after we've got Mrs Sweetman a cup of tea.'

'Oh, thank you, dear. I could do with one after all that waiting.'

Sam carefully carried a plate of biscuits over to Mrs Sweetman and offered her one. He was duly thanked, and then they were free. Ethan hurried Sam through the hall and out of the fire doors at the side before anyone else could buttonhole them. The village had known his every move practically since he had been born. Now that he was a young widower with a child, its elders seemed intent on engaging him in conversation whenever they saw him to fend off any possibility of loneliness. It was kind, and a gesture that Ethan had appreciated when Jenna had first died. But he'd come to terms with being alone now, and this afternoon there was somewhere else he needed to be.

On the grass in a semi-circle, large, open-sided tents shaded the dogs and their owners from the sun. The police were there, along with a stand for hearing dogs and one for guide dogs. The mountain rescue dogs were at the far end, and Ethan wondered whether he would have to work through all the rest before he got to see Kate.

Sam saved him the trouble, running across the grass towards her. She was wearing a red T-shirt, with the mountain rescue insignia, and when she saw Sam she stretched her arms out in an expression of joy that made Ethan's heart thump in his chest.

He saw Sam hug her. He didn't often do that, saving his hugs for people he really liked. A little quiver of foreboding—the thought that he shouldn't let Sam become dependent on her hugs—was forgotten as he saw Sam's face when one of the men Kate was with issued a command to his dog and the animal trotted over to Sam, holding out its paw. Ethan saw Kate nod to Sam and he took the dog's paw and shook hands.

She looked up and saw Ethan. This time she didn't stretch her arms out, but her smile was no less broad.

'You made it, then.'

'Yes. We made it.'

He knew that Kate was perfectly capable of smiling through the most challenging problems. He'd fallen for her cover-up himself, believing that she was coping well with the after-effects of the attack, but he fancied that he was beginning to see a little more clearly now. And this afternoon, she had a lightness about her that convinced him her joy was genuine.

'Looks as if we have a budding dog trainer here.' She grinned over at Sam who was being introduced to each of the dogs in turn.

'I'm hoping so. We'll need to commit to some classes when the puppy's old enough.'

Ethan smiled across at one of Kate's companions and Mike strode over to shake his hand.

'Ethan. How are you doing? I haven't see you in a while.'

'I'm good. I've been busy.' It occurred to Ethan that he'd slowly withdrawn from village life over the last year, intent on proving to himself that he could manage alone. Maybe he *was* lonely.

'Sam told me all about his puppy when I saw him the other day with your father. Where *is* George?' Mike looked around.

'He'll be along later. He's taking Mum over to her tailoring class first.' The tailoring class was actually an excuse to sit around, drink tea and talk. His mother had been attending it for ten years now, which meant she'd probably learned just about all she needed to know about the sewing part of the afternoon.

'Well, I'll let you have a look around. Kate, you've got the leaflets?'

'Yes.' Kate picked up a pile of leaflets from the table behind her and handed one to Ethan. 'Here you are.'

'Thanks.' Ethan knew all about the activities of the mountain rescuers, but he took the leaflet anyway, its value growing in inverse proportion to its usefulness, because Kate had given it to him.

'I'm in there...' She grinned and pointed out a small figure, standing with a group of others. 'I'll mention that because you wouldn't be able to recognise me otherwise.'

Maybe not. Maybe it was just his imagination that he'd recognise the way she held herself anywhere. 'Do you go out with the team?'

'Yes, I've completed my training and I'm a fully fledged mountain rescuer now. Even got the T-shirt.' She pointed at the logo on her shirt, and Ethan tried not to stare. The thin material draped over her curves looked great.

'But you don't handle any of the dogs?' Each dog responded only to the commands of one of the men.

'No, the dogs live with their handlers, and I didn't want to leave an animal alone while I was at work. I decided it was best to just help with them. And be a part of the team when we go out, of course.'

This meant a lot to Kate. She was all about the challenge, and the more he saw that the more he knew she could challenge her own demons if she just had the right tools to do it with. And, even though he'd decided to leave that to Usha, he couldn't help wanting to be a part of it.

'Come and say hello.' She turned to the men, who were now showing Sam the different commands that the dogs would respond to. 'I'm going to do some leafleting in a moment. That police sniffer-spaniel may be gorgeous, but he's getting all the attention.'

The afternoon seemed to go well. The sun shone and the old church hadn't seen so many people pass its doors in years. The mountain rescue team was busy, talking to people and showing them how they worked with the dogs. Sam had been sniffed by the spaniel and had watched a hearing-assistance dog nudge at its owner's hand when a bell was rung. Then, when Ethan's father had arrived, keen to see the display, he'd done it all again with him.

Ethan couldn't take his eyes off Kate. She was bright, smiling, always in the midst of people. In the end, he gave in to temptation, walked back to the mountain rescue stand and was promptly pressed into handing out leaflets.

'So where's mine, then?' His father's voice sounded behind him.

'Here you are.' Ethan handed him a leaflet. 'Make sure you read it carefully. Lots of good information.'

'Will do.' His father's eyes twinkled with quiet humour.

'Hello. Welcome!' Kate appeared, holding her hand out towards his father. This was the routine they'd fallen into. Leaflet first and then a greeting from Kate, who introduced visitors to the other members of the team so they could talk and ask questions.

'Hello. I'm George.' His father grinned, shaking her hand. 'I know your friend here.'

Ethan rolled his eyes. 'He's my father. Dad, this is Kate… Where's Sam?'

'Over there.' His father pointed to the next stand, which was taking kids in groups of six to show them how guide dogs negotiated a busy road. Ethan looked and counted only five heads.

He looked around but couldn't see Sam. Suddenly the safety of the village crumbled and panic tore at his heart. Sam *had* to be here somewhere. His father and Kate were looking too, Kate climbing up on a chair so that she could see over the heads of the people.

'There!' Ethan felt Kate's hand nudge his shoulder. 'There he is.'

Sam was walking towards them around the perimeter of the church hall. He seemed a little distracted, as if he didn't quite know where he was going. Then Ethan heard Kate catch her breath and she jumped down from the chair and started to run towards Sam. He'd just wiped his hands down the front of his white T-shirt, leaving a trail of blood.

Ethan reached Sam first, coming to a halt in front of his son and kneeling down. 'Sam? Show me your hands, mate.'

Sam held out his hands palms upwards. 'There's a man, Dad.'

'Did he hurt you?' The fear was like nothing he'd ever felt before.

'It's not his blood, Ethan.' Kate's voice beside him was calm and quiet. She was right. Sam's hands were smeared with blood, but there was no injury.

He had to get the T-shirt off him. If he pulled it over Sam's head it would smear blood all over his face, and Ethan had no idea where the blood had come from. He pulled his keys from his pocket, pushing them into the material to make a hole, then tearing the T-shirt all the way up the front so that Kate could slip it from his shoulders.

His own shirt was open over a T-shirt, and Ethan pulled it off his shoulders and wrapped it around Sam. The boy snuggled into it.

'There's a man, Dad.'

'What man? Is he bleeding?' Ethan had quickly examined Sam's chest and arms and there wasn't a mark on him. Just the blood on his hands, most of which had been smeared on the front of his T-shirt.

'He's over there…' Sam pointed behind him to the corner of the church hall. Then he wound his arms around Ethan's neck, clinging to him. His only two options were leaving Sam here on his own, or taking him with him to go and see, and both tore at him.

'I'll go.' Kate must have seen his hesitation and was already on her feet, jogging towards the spot that Sam had indicated. Fearless as always. Ethan hugged Sam tight, watching her go.

CHAPTER EIGHT

THE CORNER OF the church hall was shaded by trees and the strip of land which lay beyond that, between the back of the building and the fence, felt secluded from the noise and bustle around the stands. Three feet in front of her, a man's body lay motionless, blood pooling around his shoulders onto the hard-baked ground.

Ethan obviously carried a great deal of guilt over not having been there when his wife needed him and he couldn't bring himself to leave Sam now. But he'd never forgive himself if he didn't tend to the injured man. She ran back to them.

'Ethan. Let your father take Sam. You have to come.'

He hesitated for one more agonising moment. 'Now, Ethan!' Kate issued the command, hoping that it gave him no choice. If she was wrong, then he could challenge her over it later.

Ethan shouted for his father, then transferred Sam into George's arms, telling him quickly to make sure all the blood was cleaned off him. As Ethan ran back towards her, she called to Mike, asking him to send someone from the police stand over with a first-aid kit, and then followed Ethan.

He dropped to his knees next to the man, all his attention now focussed on him. 'He's alive. I have a pulse.' Ethan's voice was quiet, concentrated, as he examined the man for injuries.

Kate looked up, trying to see what might have happened, in case that could help. 'He must have fallen from the roof. The gutter's broken and the fence has been smashed.'

Ethan nodded, his face grave. 'Call an ambulance. Tell them that a doctor's in attendance and we need them as soon as possible.'

'I'll get my phone.' She'd left it in her jacket pocket, back on the stand.

'Take mine.' Ethan handed her his phone and continued his examination, moving the man as little as possible so as not to further injure him.

'He's unconscious, probably fallen from a height of thirty feet. One of the fence palings has gone almost all the way through his leg below the knee. His airways are clear, pulse is very weak. His chest seems uninjured but… stomach's hard and distended.'

Kate knew that wasn't good. She relayed the

details on to the ambulance controller. 'Anything else?'

'Can you pass me the phone, please?'

Ethan was very calm, very cool. That was more worrying than anything, because Kate knew full well that this was his reaction to the seriousness of the situation. He spoke quickly into the phone and she stared at the man's face. He was young, maybe not even twenty. Kate hoped that Ethan was receiving the assurances that he needed and that help would come soon.

She bent, laying her fingers gently on the man's brow, murmuring into his ear. 'Hold on. We're here for you.'

'That's right.' Ethan's voice beside her. 'Keep talking to him.'

The realisation that this was all she could do hit Kate and she blinked back her tears. If the man seemed unresponsive then maybe something she said might register. If that was the case, then she had to choose her words carefully.

She spoke as clearly as she could, telling the man that he was loved. That a doctor was here, and he had to hold on. Then again, there was no way of knowing when and if he might drift back into consciousness.

'Give me your hand.' She stretched her hand out, and Ethan guided it to a spot on the man's leg just above the knee. 'Press hard…harder.

Good. That's right. Keep that up, you're doing just fine.'

She was so frightened of making a mistake that could cost a life. But Ethan would tell her what to do. The police dog-handler arrived back with the first-aid kit, kneeling down next to them and opening it, following Ethan's calm, quiet instructions.

Scissors, to cut the leg of the man's jeans. Dressings. The policeman handed over what Ethan needed and he started to pack around the wound, taping it tightly to stop the bleeding.

'Okay, I think we have it. Kate, release the pressure…good. Clean your hands and put a pair of gloves on.'

There was no blood on her hands but she cleaned them anyway. She heard Ethan ask if there was a cervical collar in the first-aid kit, and the policeman looked helplessly through its contents.

'There.' She picked up the collar, tearing the wrappings, and gave it to Ethan.

'Thanks. Can you find his pulse?'

'Yes.' She felt the man's wrist, feeling the faint rhythm of his heart under her fingers. 'Got it.'

'Okay, tell me if it weakens.'

She couldn't. She didn't know enough. But Ethan had no one else here to help him, and she had to. She knew how to do this, even if she'd only done it with animals before.

Ethan was working quickly and carefully, his attention now centred on the man's stomach and chest. 'Go round to the front and make sure the ambulance knows where we are. There's another doctor on his way too.'

Kate looked up, wondering if he was sending her away, but he was talking to the policeman, who got to his feet, leaving quickly. They were on their own now, and Ethan was trusting her to help him.

It was quiet here. She watched as Ethan carefully probed the man's stomach, causing a weak moan to escape his lips.

'It's all right. Just hold on, the doctor's here…' She started to talk again, taking care to keep her fingers over the man's pulse. She saw Ethan nod, but the man seemed not to have heard her and was unresponsive again. All the same, she kept talking.

Then, sudden activity. One of the policemen was ushering a man in a high-visibility jacket towards them.

'Ethan.' The man set his bag down on the ground. He obviously knew Ethan, and Ethan's tight smile told Kate that this was the help that they so needed.

'John, thanks for coming. You have the REBOA kit?'

'Yes.' John knelt down next to Ethan, and Kate saw the identification flash on his jacket: 'Doctor'.

Ethan was quickly updating John about the man's condition and John was nodding. They seemed to be coming to a quick, unspoken agreement about what should happen next. 'You've done this more times than me, Ethan. You lead.'

REBOA.... REBOA...? Kate had heard those initials before, although they weren't a part of animal medicine. It was a last resort, something only available for treating people.

John opened his bag and Ethan turned to Kate. 'We'll need your help with this.'

'Yes. Just tell me what to do.'

There were plenty of people here who had basic medical training with the police and the mountain rescue team. Ethan must have anticipated this course of action, and he could have sent her away and chosen someone else. Kate had no doubt that he would have done, if it had been in his patient's best interests.

But, despite all her weakness, he'd chosen her. She wouldn't let him down, and she wouldn't let their patient down either.

Ethan was disinfecting his hands as best he

could with wipes from the medical kit. John was laying out what they needed. Kate waited.

'Can you cut a little further across the leg of his jeans?' Ethan had already undone the waist-band and zip to examine the man's stomach. 'I need access to the femoral artery—you know where that is?

'Yes, I know.' She could do this. Animal patients tended to wriggle a great deal more than human ones, and Kate could cut a dressing off almost anything. A pair of jeans was a piece of cake, but when Ethan handed her a pair of surgical scissors she cut as carefully as if she were doing this for the first time.

'That's great.' Ethan didn't look at her—he and John were both busy with their own preparations—but his voice imputed that she really had done well. Kate breathed a sigh of relief.

She remembered what REBOA was now. A line was inserted into the femoral artery and a small balloon manoeuvred into place along the artery. When it was inflated, it would stem internal bleeding, in either the chest or the abdomen.

It was demanding work, and a technique of last resort even in controlled surroundings. Here it could only be contemplated if both doctors believed that their patient couldn't survive the ten-mile journey to the hospital without it.

Ethan was carefully inserting the catheter, the first part of the delicate process. His posture was relaxed, but his concentration was so focussed and intense that he probably wouldn't have noticed if the weather turned suddenly and it began to snow.

Ethan and John worked together, exchanging quiet instructions and updates. Kate kept her eyes on the blood-pressure monitor, praying that the falling stats might soon change. She held sterile lines clear of the ground, took pieces of equipment and then gave them back again exactly as instructed. If Ethan had told her to stop breathing, she would have done it.

'Nice.' John's one word as Ethan sat back on his heels was the only indicator of hope but Kate would take it.

Ethan was busying himself with the patient, and John shot her a smile. 'You did well. We can manage now if you want to go and change your T-shirt…'

Her T-shirt was spattered with blood. But Ethan had given her a job to do, and Kate wanted to see it through. 'May I just hold his hand, until the ambulance gets here? I won't get in the way.'

Ethan looked up suddenly. 'You've earned that.'

Kate took the young man's hand with trembling fingers. She'd earned her place here, and he was going to allow her to stay.

CHAPTER NINE

WHEN THE TWO-MAN ambulance crew arrived, she was in the way, and she had to go. Not waiting for John or Ethan to tell her so, she stepped back, walking towards the policeman who was stationed at the corner of the hall, stopping anyone from approaching.

'Kate. Kate!' Mike was standing as close as he was allowed, holding a blanket and her zip-up sweatshirt. Kate ignored the blanket, zipping the sweatshirt around her and wriggling out of her T-shirt.

'Nice trick.' Mike grinned as she pulled the T-shirt over her head and threaded her arms into the sweatshirt. 'You're going to have to tell me how you do that.'

Kate smirked at him. 'Women's secrets.'

'Yeah. I'd figured that one out. How is he?'

'I don't really know, but it seems pretty bad. Ethan and the other doctor have done a surgical procedure.'

'Really.' Mike nodded. He'd been Kate's mentor when she'd first joined the mountain rescue team two years ago. He knew better than anyone that doctors waited to do surgery at hospital if it was at all possible. 'We'll just have to hope for the best then.'

'Is Sam still here?'

'No, his grandfather's taken him home. He had a bit of a shock but once he was cleaned up he seemed all right. We gave him one of the kids' T-shirts.'

'That's nice.' They only had a few of those, and they'd been saving them. But Sam deserved one.

'One of the police dog handlers came over with a children's activity pack as well. We all made a bit of a fuss of him and he cheered up.'

Kate knew that the guys would have done their best to lift Sam's spirits. They all had children of their own, and knew that Ethan couldn't be there for his son. She wondered how he was going to feel about that, when this was all over.

'Is Ethan going to the hospital?' Mike broke into her thoughts.

'I don't know. Do you have another T-shirt? Ethan got the worst of the blood spillage.'

'Yep, no problem. Wait here, I'll bring it to you.'

She waited for five minutes, knowing that

Ethan would come as soon as he could. He would want to know that Sam was all right. When he finally appeared, he made straight for her.

'He's still in a bad way, but you helped give him a chance, Kate.'

It took five seconds to say it. But it was five seconds in which Ethan could have asked about Sam, and he'd chosen to tell her what she needed to hear. She proffered the T-shirt with trembling hands.

'Sam's okay. Your dad cleaned him up and everyone made a big fuss of him. They've gone home.'

'Thanks.' Ethan stripped off his T-shirt, dropping it onto the ground.

Wow. The way Ethan filled a shirt, it had been impossible to conclude that he didn't have a good body. The reality of it exceeded Kate's expectations. And she shouldn't be thinking that, because there were much more important things to concentrate on.

'You're going to the hospital?'

'Yes.' He pulled his phone from his jeans pocket and handed it to her. 'Would you be able to take my dad's number and call him, let him know? Tell him I'll be there as soon as I can and ask him to text me and let me know how Sam is.'

'Yes, of course.' He was trusting her with this, too.

'He's under "d"—for Dad.' One corner of Ethan's mouth twitched and Kate realised that she was staring at him. He took the clean T-shirt from her and pulled it over his head. Too late. Ethan wasn't someone you could un-see in a hurry.

He was looking over his shoulder, back to where John and the ambulance crew were carefully transferring the young man onto a stretcher. Kate found the number, transferring it into her own phone and checking it.

'Got to go…' For a moment, Ethan was still, his gaze locked onto her face. Then he turned and was gone.

The ambulance left, and she called George, letting him know where Ethan was, and receiving assurances that Sam was fine and that he'd text Ethan and let him know. And then there was nothing more for Kate to do. Mike shooed her away from the mountain rescue stand, which was rapidly being packed up and dismantled, telling her to go and get a cup of tea.

'You want a decent cup. Not a couple of mouthfuls.' The middle-aged woman who had been busy wrapping uneaten biscuits in cling-film ignored the cups and saucers that were still laid out on the tea table and reached underneath it, producing a mug.

'Thanks. You're a lifesaver.'

'From what I hear, you and Ethan Conway are lifesavers.' The woman smiled at her and Kate shivered. Hearing herself and Ethan mentioned in the same sentence was new, and oddly exciting. 'How is the young man?'

'I don't really know. He's on his way to hospital and Ethan's gone with him. He says that he has a chance.'

'Good.' The woman produced a hip flask from her pocket. 'Would you like some of this to go with it, love?'

'What is it?'

'Nice drop of brandy. Only, don't tell the vicar. Church premises….'

There was no particular reason why she should find it incongruous that the tea ladies were surreptitiously downing brandy in the church kitchen, but it made Kate smile all the same.

'I bet you can do with a drink after serving this many cups of tea.'

'That's for sure.' The woman reached for two teacups and poured a splash into the bottom of each, handing Kate one. 'I'm Pat. Here's to a happy ending.'

Kate grinned. 'Kate. To happy endings.'

They clinked their cups together, and Pat downed the contents of hers in one. Kate followed suit, almost choking as the astringent heat hit the back of her throat.

'Oh...!' Pat's eyes had filled with tears, and she blinked them away. 'I'm not used to this. But it's a bit of a tradition here, once we get the dishwasher stacked.'

Kate sat down with a bump on one of the chairs next to the tea table, her head swimming. 'Maybe I should have sipped it.'

'Me too. So much for bravado.' Pat reached for another mug and filled both with tea, pushing Kate's towards her.

'Here's to bravado, then.' Kate grinned, taking a welcome mouthful of tea.

'Yes, that's much better.' Pat sat down, looking at Kate speculatively. 'You know Ethan, then?'

'Yes. I'm a vet. I looked after his dog, Jeff.'

Pat nodded. 'Poor old Jeff. Great big thing but as gentle as they come. When Sam was little he used to sit himself down next to his pushchair, nudging anyone he didn't know away if they got too close. Jenna used to have to lean on him, to get him to move.'

'You knew Ethan's wife?' It seemed somehow presumptuous to use her name.

'Oh, yes, she came from around here. And

she was often in the village. She used to bring Sam to see his grandparents. Such a shame. If there were ever two people that belonged together…'

Kate took a swallow of her tea. For a short time it had seemed that *she* and Ethan belonged together. But she knew so little about Ethan, and if the people he'd grown up with said he belonged with someone else then it must be true.

'Sam seems… He's got a great relationship with his dad.'

'Yes, he has. And Ethan's devoted to him. Chocolate biscuit?'

'Yes, please. Can I take it with me? I should get back to our stand. I'm sure there's something I can help with.' Kate managed a smile as Pat stripped the cling-film off one of the plates and wrapped three biscuits, putting them into her hand.

'There you go, my love.'

She wandered outside, sitting down on the steps outside the front of the hall. Her car was still in the garage, and Mike had said he'd drop her home, but he was nowhere to be seen.

Ethan had trusted her. It made her feel good… no, better than good. It had made her feel strong, as if his belief in her was worth more than anyone else's. But he'd gone now.

Of course he had. If he hadn't needed to go to

the hospital, then he would have gone straight to Sam. They were priorities, and it would be unthinkable to expect anything different. And if she allowed herself to rely on him too much, then she would be just setting herself up for heartbreak.

She picked up her tea, wandering over to the empty mountain rescue tent. Sitting around drinking tea was all very well, but taking the tent down was the kind of problem she needed to distract her right now. At least that involved some possibility of success.

In the cramped space inside the ambulance, Ethan and John had managed to prevent their patient from bleeding out, or having a seizure, or a heart attack, or any one of a number of things that could have killed him before they reached the hospital.

Time had become an irrelevance, something that might be counted on a clock somewhere, but which didn't matter. An hour or a minute. It didn't make any difference as long as his patient was still alive and there was one more thing that he could do to keep him that way.

He'd made it to the resuscitation room. Then he'd made it past the concentrated activity which assessed his injuries and vital signs. He'd been stabilised, and Ethan had made the decision that he was ready for surgery. And then Ethan had finally looked at his watch.

He checked his phone and saw the text from his father, saying that Sam was all right. Then he spent ten minutes under the shower, knowing that he couldn't speak to Sam just yet. In a moment he'd be able to be a father again, instead of a doctor whose one aim was to keep the patient under his care alive.

'Hey, Sam. How are you doing?'

'You made the man better, Dad?'

'Yes, we did.' Surely he was allowed this one little lie, to reassure Sam?

'He had lots of blood on him.'

'Yes, I know. Were you frightened?'

'Yes.' Sam suddenly sounded subdued.

'I'll bet you were. It was a frightening thing to happen to you, and you were very brave to come and find us the way you did.'

'Did he have some blood left?'

'Yes, he had plenty of blood left. We gave him some extra as well. He's all right now.'

'Okay…'

Sam chattered on to him, and Ethan sat in the doctor's rest room, letting the tightly coiled spring in his chest loosen a little. Reminding himself that he'd made sure that Sam was well looked after.

He promised Sam that he'd be back soon,

and then spoken briefly to his father. Then he called Kate.

'Ethan.' She sounded pleased that he'd called.

'Hi. I just wanted you to know that…he's made it into surgery.'

A puffed-out breath of relief. 'Thank you. That's really great. I suppose you don't know anything else yet?'

'No, but he's a fighter. That helps.' Kate would understand that. She was a fighter too.

'Well, that's good to know. Where are you?'

'At the hospital still. My dad's coming to pick me up and I'll fetch my car and then go and get Sam.'

'I'd better let you go. Thanks so much for taking the time to call.' She seemed about to hang up, now.

'Wait.' There was something more he had to say. And even if there hadn't been he could still spare these few moments, just to talk to her. 'I wanted to say that I'm sorry. For rushing off like that.'

He heard her expel a sharp breath. 'Right. Because there was nowhere you needed to go. Don't be crazy, Ethan.'

'How about, sorry that I left you to find him.'

'No, that one doesn't wash either. You were making sure that Sam wasn't hurt. That's your first priority, Ethan.'

He'd been clinging to Sam, blinded to everything other than the fact that he needed his son to be all right. Kate had jerked him back out of that, and made him see what he needed to do.

'I'm glad you think that I thought about it so rationally.'

'You're allowed to be irrational. Goes with the territory.'

Ethan chuckled. Just the sound of her voice was making him feel that somehow he'd managed to cover all the bases. Look after Sam, be a doctor… Maybe even look after Kate a little.

'Sam tells me he wants to be a mountain rescue volunteer when he grows up.'

'Does he? That's nice.'

'Yeah. And he wants to train his dog to shake hands.'

'That can be arranged. I'm an expert at getting dogs to shake hands.' She caught her breath suddenly, as if she'd said something she shouldn't. 'If you can't find anyone else, that is…'

The thought that maybe he should find someone else, someone who Sam wouldn't be tempted to accept as a mother figure, had occurred to Ethan. But right now he just wanted to feel life pumping in his veins, and Kate made him feel alive.

'Since you're the expert, it would be very bad manners to even think there was anyone else.'

She laughed and Ethan began to wish that he could touch her. Just to hold her for a moment and celebrate the warmth of life.

'You took a chance on me. When you asked me to help.' Her voice took on a note of tension, as if this was something that she'd been waiting to say.

'No, I didn't. You were as steady as a rock. I had no worries on that score. You know, don't you, that if I'd had any doubts I would have had no choice but to ask someone else to help.'

'Yes, I know. The patient's needs come first.' Her voice lightened a little, as if she half-believed what he'd just said.

'You're stronger than you think, Kate.'

'And how strong do you think I think I am? Or do you think that I think that you think—?'

Ethan's laugh cut her short. 'Stop. You lost me on the second "think". I'm going to go now, before you reduce my brain to mush.'

'Yes, you'd better. Give Sam a hug from me.'

Maybe he would. Just maybe…

Ethan went to check on the young man on Monday morning before he started work and then visited him every day after that. For the first three days he was in the intensive care ward.

His mother had told Ethan that he was only nineteen, and that his name was Christopher but that his friends called him CK, because those were his initials.

On the fourth day, CK opened his eyes and focussed blearily on Ethan's face. Then, on day six, he told him that he'd climbed up on the roof for a bet, but that he'd learned his lesson. He remembered nothing of the incident or the minutes before it.

It would be a long journey for CK. He had significant internal injuries, and he would have to learn to walk again, after his leg had been shattered by the fence paling. But against all the odds he'd survived and was making a recovery. Ethan always tried to follow up on his patients and often the outcome wasn't such a good one. But somehow CK's hold on life seemed like a miracle.

CHAPTER TEN

THE PART OF the week that Kate had occupied wasn't all that significant time-wise. Short phone calls to update her on CK's progress, and an hour one evening with Sam, taking him to see his puppy. But for all that, when his mind wasn't concentrated on work, Kate had occupied the greater part of Ethan's attention.

He had little enough to offer her—a scarred heart that still didn't know whether it was strong enough to love any more than it already had. Limited time and a schedule of early mornings that didn't fit in all that well with Kate's schedule at the veterinary surgery. He should keep in contact, try to be there for her if she needed him, but leave it at that.

Then, on Friday afternoon, he got a call. His father put Sam on the line, who explained that he had an important project on hand with Grandpa, and that he wanted to stay the night there. As soon as Ethan put his phone back down on his desk, he changed his mind and picked it up again, dialling Kate's number.

'I've got a free evening, as Sam's staying at my parents. I thought I might catch a film and wondered if you'd like to keep me company?' In other words, this wasn't a date.

'Yes, that sounds great. Do you know what's on?'

He'd forgotten to look. 'No.'

'Hang on a minute, let me get to my desk.' He heard the sound of Kate's footsteps, and then the chime as a computer was nudged into life. 'Here we are. There's a romance, but it's only got one star on the reviews. Gritty story of cops on the beat… Superheroes… Um…oh, and there's one in Chinese, with subtitles.'

None of that sounded particularly promising, but that wasn't really the point. 'What do you fancy?'

'I don't really know. What do you think?'

There was a short silence and they both laughed together. 'All right. I'll go first. I'm quite partial to superheroes, actually.'

Ethan chuckled. Why did that not surprise him? 'Me too. I heard that one was pretty good.'

'Yes it's got four-and-a-half stars. Unless you want to go and see it with Sam?'

'I think the one that's currently out is a bit grown up for Sam.'

'Oh, yes, so it is. What do you think, then? There are showings at eight, nine and half-past nine.'

'I'll pick you up at half-eight, then?'

The smell of popcorn and a woman standing next to him in the queue for tickets. Ethan hadn't done this for a while. But Kate was just a friend. They were two people, neither of whom had anyone to go to the cinema with, and who didn't want to go alone.

As they got to the head of the queue, her phone buzzed. Ethan selected the seats and was about to pay for them when suddenly Kate slammed her hand onto the debit-card reader.

'I'll get them.'

'No.' When he glanced across at her, Kate was frowning. This didn't seem like the usual squabble over who paid for tickets. She grabbed his arm, pulling him to one side, apologising to the woman behind the desk, who rolled her eyes.

'I've got a call out. Mountain rescue. Ethan, I'm sorry.'

That was usually his line—called away for an emergency somewhere. He knew just how bad Kate must be feeling at the moment, and was surprised to find that he wasn't angry in the least. He'd always assumed that other people's protestations, that it was all right and that he really must go, were just good manners.

'What's happened?' Ethan began to walk towards the exit doors.

'It's an old couple. Apparently they went to visit their daughter in the next village this afternoon and she saw them onto the bus home. But they never arrived. They searched everywhere and, when it began to get late, they called for help. The bus goes through…' She consulted her phone. 'How do you say that?'

'Coleswittam. The double "t" is sounded as "th".'

Kate raised her eyebrows. 'Right. That's sure to help a poor, confused Londoner find it. Do you know it?'

'Yes, it's to the west of here. Quite a tourist spot in the summer—hill-walking country with caves and a few waterfalls. It's very beautiful, but not the kind of place an elderly couple should be at night.'

Kate quirked the corners of her mouth down. 'It doesn't sound like it. I'm so sorry, Ethan.'

'Nonsense. Do you want a hand?'

She stopped so suddenly that Ethan almost bumped into her. 'Well…are you sure?'

'A doctor might come in useful.'

'Well, we hope not, but…' Kate started walking again. 'Let's go, then.'

* * *

Ethan drove to his house first, and Kate waited outside while he quickly found a pair of walking boots, stuffing them into a rucksack along with a waterproof jacket. He put his medical bag into the boot of the car and they drove to her cottage to pick up her gear. Then he took the short cut along a dirt track to Coleswittam.

'Is everyone at the Old Ford?'

'Yes, that's the meeting point.' The car got to the brow of a hill and she pointed ahead of them. 'There they are.'

The group of men and women seemed well organised. A sandy-haired man who was obviously in charge was splitting everyone up into search parties and showing them which area they should cover on the map. Kate walked towards him and he smiled.

'Thanks for coming.' His gaze flipped towards Ethan.

'This is Ethan Conway. He's a doctor. Ethan, this is Grant, our team leader.'

'Good to have you on board, Ethan.' Grant shook his hand firmly. 'Kate, I want you and Ethan to go with Mike. You should know that the husband has dementia, so he may have wandered off somewhere and got lost. His wife might be looking for him. We don't know. I want you to go up to the Kettle—Mike knows where that is—and maybe Maisie can get a scent there.'

The Kettle. Ethan had played there himself when he was a kid, and in the summer it was a great place to bathe, to explore the rocks and caves which surrounded the pool. At night, and with the weather closing in, it wasn't somewhere he'd want anyone to be lost and alone.

Kate nodded. 'I've got flashlights. Do you have a spare hard hat for Ethan, in case we need to go into the caves?'

'Back of my truck. We have a medical kit too.' Grant flashed a querying glance at Ethan.

'That's okay, I have my own in the car.'

'Great. Good luck, then. Keep in touch.'

'Will do.' Kate hurried over to the open back of an SUV, which bore the logo of the mountain rescue team, leaning in to find what she wanted. Then she joined Ethan as he transferred the contents of his medical bag into his rucksack. Mike joined them, leading Maisie, his dog, and Kate bent to greet the Border collie with a pat on the head.

'Maisie will find them if anyone can. She never gives up.'

Ethan was sure she was right. He knew that no one would stop looking until the elderly couple was found, but it was a matter of time, as well. An elderly couple might not survive a night out in these hills.

They walked away from the circle of car headlights into the gloom, only flashlights to light their way. After the heat of a summer's day the evening was cool and the spattering of rain on Ethan's face would have been refreshing if it wasn't another worry to add to all the others for the missing couple.

'Oh!' They'd walked in near silence for half an hour, concentrating on the uneven ground at their feet, and Kate's quiet exclamation as she stumbled sounded somehow louder.

'Okay?' He caught her arm, steadying her.

'Yes, thanks.' She stopped, shining the flashlight around her, and Mike bent to Maisie, taking a plastic bag out of his pocket which contained a folded item of clothing.

'No scent yet?' Kate's words were more of an observation than a question. They'd know when Maisie caught a scent of the old couple.

'Maybe she'll get one a little further on.' Mike fondled Maisie's head briefly and got to his feet.

'Another three quarters of an hour to the Kettle?' Ethan knew these hills well, but the darkness was disorientating.

'Yep. Bit less, maybe.' Mike pointed the beam of his flashlight in the direction they were going in and started walking.

'You know this area?' He heard Kate's quiet voice next to him.

'Yes. I spent half my time out here when I was a kid. It's a bit different at night though.'

At night. A thought struck him suddenly and he called to Mike. 'The couple we're looking for. They're local?'

'Yes, lived here all their lives.'

'Then they'll know the Kettle, right? We're headed for the east side, but on the west side...'

Mike stopped suddenly, scratching his head. 'Yeah. You're right. I'll call Grant and suggest we take the western approach.'

'What?' He could see Kate's eyes, wide in the darkness, looking up at him.

'Anyone who's lived here all their lives will know that the place for couples is the west side of the Kettle. The east side's a lot prettier, and that's where the walkers and tourists go. On the west side, there are caves and a bit more privacy.'

'And you think that they would go there—like a courting couple?'

'Maybe. Makes sense to me that they might. We used to come up here in the evenings all the time, when we were teenagers.'

Mike ended his call, putting his phone back into his pocket. 'Okay, Grant agrees. We'll go this way.' Mike shone his torch up an incline, and they made their way over the rough, stony ground.

'Surely they couldn't have managed this?' Kate was stumbling in the darkness, and Ethan took her hand to steady her. When she regained her balance she kept hold of him, her fingers warm in his.

'There's another way round, much flatter and easier to walk. If they knew where they were headed, then they could have taken that route.' Ethan remembered that there was a bus stop too, along the road on that side of the hill.

'You think they knew where they were headed? It must have been a long time since they did any courting.'

'For someone with dementia, those memories of their youth become more vivid, as the intervening memories fade. They often recreate their early memories, because they seem more real to them.'

'And *you* used to come here? Was it where you first kissed a girl?' It seemed that, despite the rugged terrain, Kate still had enough breath left to tease him.

'Yes. That was a very long time ago...'

Ethan heard Mike laugh and remembered suddenly that he and Kate weren't alone, however much it felt that she was the only other person in the world right now.

'Me and the wife used to go there, too. Her father didn't think too much of me.' Mike remarked.

There was no more possibility of talk as they toiled up the hill, but Kate kept her hand in Ethan's.

They were keeping up a punishing pace, uphill and in the darkness. But Ethan's dark presence beside her, his hand to guide her, was helping Kate keep up with the two men.

Then the terrain levelled out, onto what seemed to be a wide causeway. Easy to traverse, it seemed a lot more likely that an elderly couple might come this way.

A sudden bark from Maisie and a quiet exclamation from Mike. 'She's got the scent.'

Maisie ran ahead, the lead playing out behind her, and Mike quickened his pace to follow. Ethan broke into a jog and Kate followed him, keeping her eyes on the ground in front of them, which was lit by the beam of his torch.

'There. Up ahead….' Ethan grabbed her hand, switching off his torch, and in the darkness Kate could see… She wasn't quite sure what she saw. A faint glimmer, maybe, in the darkness.

'Yes! I see it.' Mike's voice. Maisie had disappeared ahead of him in the darkness, but Kate could hear her short, sharp barks indicating that she was following a scent.

The grass gave way to smooth rocks, and they scrambled across them. The light was becoming stronger now, yellowish, not white like the light from their torches. Mike was reeling in Maisie's lead and Ethan led Kate across the boulders in their way, into the mouth of a small cave, the rocks around them smooth and rounded.

Kate gasped. There was a fire, well-built and burning brightly. Beside it sat an old man, and on the other side a woman was lying, covered with a couple of coats. And the man was waving a burning brand from the fire, as if to fend them off.

Maisie trotted over to Mike, sitting at his feet, and he gave her a reward from his pocket. Ethan was suddenly still, holding on to Kate's arm to stop her from approaching the man.

'Hello. You must be Mr Fuller.' His voice was quiet, without any of the urgency that all three of the searchers were feeling.

'What are you doing in my house? You're not my son.' Fred Fuller waved the branch ferociously, obviously confused and angry.

'No, I'm his friend. Ethan.'

'And is this your girl?' Fred pointed at Kate, seeming a little mollified by Ethan's words.

'Yes, that's right Mr Fuller.' Kate smiled, disengaging herself from Ethan's grip, and stepping forward. 'I'm Kate.'

'Let's take a look at you, then.' Fred lowered the branch, putting it down onto the rock floor of the cave.

She walked towards him, kneeling down beside him, and Fred peered at her face. Out of the corner of her eye, she saw Ethan behind her, quietly sliding the burning branch away from Fred's reach.

'You must be cold, Mr Fuller.' Fred was wearing a shirt and tie, with a V-necked sweater, but his coat was covering his wife. 'I've got a cup of tea.'

Fred brightened visibly. 'Yes, we could do with a cup of tea. Eh, Edie?'

'Is Mrs Fuller all right?' Edie Fuller seemed to be asleep, and Ethan was working his way round to take a look at her.

'She's…' Fred shrugged. 'What's he doing?'

'My…boyfriend's a doctor.' Kate kept the subterfuge up, feeling herself blush. 'He's going to see if Mrs Fuller's awake.'

'A doctor, eh?' Fred nodded in approval. 'You've done well for yourself, girl. Don't throw that fish back into the sea.'

Kate could feel her ears burning. But Ethan was taking advantage of Fred's sudden interest in her love life, and taking the opportunity gently to examine Edie.

'No, I won't.' She wriggled out of her backpack, opening it with one hand and pulling out the light thermal blanket. 'Here, would you like this around your shoulders?'

'What's that thing?' Fred looked at the shiny reflective blanket, pushing it away roughly. 'Where's my tea?'

'In my bag. I've got a thermos flask.'

Mike had stepped back, away from the mouth of the cave, and Kate could hear him on his phone, quietly calling their position in. There would be others here soon, but in the meantime they had to keep the old couple warm.

'I could do with a cuppa. I'm cold.' Fred's voice seemed suddenly thin and frail. Ethan turned for a moment, taking off his coat and leaving it on the ground beside him.

'What about this, then?' Kate reached forward, picking up the coat and wrapping it around Fred's shoulders. He seemed to like it a bit better than the blanket, and tried to push his arms awkwardly into the sleeves. Kate helped him, fastening the zip at the front.

'When he asks yer to marry him…' Fred leaned forward '…don't say no, now. You girls…you play hard to get and a man can get the wrong idea.'

Fred seemed to have no regard for the fact that Ethan must be able to hear every word of their conversation, and Kate wondered what he was thinking. Probably just the same as she was, that keeping Fred warm and quiet was the main thing right now.

'He hasn't asked me yet. I think he might, though.'

She pulled the flask out of her rucksack, hoping that tea might divert Fred's attention a little. Pouring a mouthful into the lid, she handed it to Fred, steadying it as he raised it to his lips.

'I can do it.' Fred glared at her but he drank his tea. 'Not much there. What are you going to say when he asks you?'

'Yes. I'll say yes. Here, have some more tea.' Kate poured another mouthful into the beaker and gave it to Fred, watching as he drank.

Ethan had his back to her. Edie wasn't moving.

CHAPTER ELEVEN

THE SMALL FIRE in the cave was burning brightly and had been well tended. Fred was obviously intent on protecting his wife, and in his confused state he could so easily have jabbed the burning branch in Kate's direction.

But she hadn't faltered. She'd calmed Fred, her smile charming the old man into allowing her to tend to him while Ethan concentrated on Edie.

Fred had done a good job there, too. His memory might be patchy, but the details of how to make a warm bed had somehow stuck. Edie was lying on a makeshift bed of soft bracken and when Ethan felt her hand it was warm under the coats.

'Edie, Edie.' He spoke to her softly and Edie didn't respond. Her pulse was strong, though, and she was breathing steadily. In the torchlight, he could see that a dark bruise was forming on the side of her face and it looked as if she'd taken a fall. Ethan didn't dare move her.

Suddenly her eyes fluttered open. 'Fred?'

'It's all right, Edie. Fred's right here.' He smoothed her tousled hair back from her face, trying to give some comfort to the old lady. It was a wonder that she and Fred had got this far and she must be confused and in pain.

'I'm Ethan, and I'm a doctor. My friend Kate is with Fred and he's okay.' Ethan wondered whether he should get his story straight with Kate's and call her his girlfriend. It was tempting. 'Are you in any pain, Edie?'

'My arm.' Edie looked up at him placidly.

'Okay, let's take a look.' He carefully moved the coats, looking at Edie's arm. It was bruised and swollen, almost certainly fractured. 'Anything else, my love?'

'No.' Edie tried to move and Ethan gently stilled her. Glancing quickly at her legs, he saw that she seemed to be able to move them without pain. That was a good sign.

'Can you do something for me? I just want you to lift your leg a little.' He put his hand gently under Edie's knee to support it. Edie obligingly lifted her leg an inch and he nodded. 'That's great. Perfect. Now the other one.'

No symptoms of a hip fracture. Edie was breathing and, when Ethan pulled his stethoscope out of his rucksack and listened to her heart, it was beating strongly.

'Are you bleeding anywhere?' The notes which Grant had handed him included a reference to Edie being on warfarin for a blood clot.

'No.' Edie's soft gaze found his. 'I know I mustn't bleed. I take warfarin, you know.'

It seemed that Edie was a lot more aware of her situation than Fred was. Ethan wondered what it might be like, knowing that they were stranded and alone and that her husband was unable to remember what they were doing here.

'Okay. I'm just going to check you over a bit. Make sure everything else is all right.'

'What about Fred?' Edie lowered her voice to a whisper. 'He can't remember, you know.'

'Yes, I know. And he's fine. Kate's looking after him. Just relax and let me look after you.'

Edie nodded, tears forming in her eyes. 'He just got off the bus and I followed him. He wanted to come here, and… I fell. He kept me warm.'

'Yeah, Fred did a good job, Edie. He looked after you really well.' Ethan turned quickly, tears blurring his eyes, and found Kate's gaze. In the flickering firelight he thought he saw her eyes bright with tears too.

'All right, Edie?' Fred was looking at his wife, his eyes tender now.

'Good enough, Fred.' Edie smiled towards her husband and he nodded, turning his attention back to the tea that Kate was holding.

'He always knows me.' Edie murmured the words quietly, and Ethan nodded, his fingers suddenly clumsy with emotion as he fumbled in his backpack for the inflatable splint.

Ethan had been so tender with Edie. He'd glanced back in Kate's direction more than once as he'd worked, a silent *'are you okay?'* and Kate had responded with a smile. Fred was confused, reacting sometimes to reality and sometimes to what was going on in his head, but he was calm now, watching Ethan tend to Edie.

'What's that?' The sound of a steady beat in the distance promised that the helicopter would be here soon.

'They're coming to take you to the hospital, Fred.' Kate wondered whether she should mention the intended mode of transport just yet.

'I want to go home. Tell them to take me home.' Fred frowned suddenly.

'Okay. But don't you think they ought to make sure that Edie's all right first?' She nodded over to where Ethan was carefully putting Edie's arm into an inflatable splint.

'She's all right.' Fred turned to Edie. 'You're all right, aren't you, girl?'

'Yes, she's going to be all right. But she needs to go to the hospital so that they can look at her arm.' Ethan turned, speaking gently but firmly.

Fred turned his mouth down, as if he wasn't quite in agreement, but wasn't going to argue. 'They'll do well to get a car up here.'

'They're sending a helicopter for you.' Ethan grinned.

'Helicopter? Hear that, Edie? We're going in a helicopter.' Fred sounded almost excited.

The paramedics took over from Ethan and he helped Kate get Fred to his feet and out of the cave. The helicopter pilot climbed down, supervising as they guided Fred into the helicopter, and strapped him in securely. It was all quickly done but Kate saw Ethan find the time to jog up to Edie's stretcher, taking her outstretched hand and bending to exchange a few words with her.

Another party of mountain rescue volunteers, who had been combing the area next to theirs, arrived and Mike went over to talk to them briefly, before re-joining Kate and Ethan.

'You must be wanting to get back for Sam.' Mike spoke to Ethan. 'The others are going now. Why don't you go with them? I'll see to the fire in the cave.'

'Sam's with my parents. I doubt they'll appreciate my turning up in the middle of the night just to stare at him while he sleeps. I'll take care of the fire. I've got to go and pack my medical things up.' Ethan was pulling his coat back on, Fred having been persuaded to give it up.

Mike grinned. 'In that case, I might go home and stare at *my* kids. Do you know the way back? If you get lost, I'm not coming out again tonight.'

Ethan chuckled. 'I know the way. My memory's not that bad.'

He glanced at Kate. A silent question, the answer to which needed no thought at all. They were a team. They stayed together.

'Sounds good. Mike, I'll go with Ethan.'

'All right. If you're sure.'

She was sure. Leaving him now was unthinkable. She watched as Mike and the other volunteers disappeared into the darkness and then walked back to the cave, where Ethan was repacking his rucksack.

Kate stuffed the unused blanket back into her own rucksack. Suddenly, after feeling that there was so much that she had to say to him, she couldn't think of a single word to say it with.

'Hey…' He sat down, poking the fire with a stick, and it flared suddenly. 'Bit of a waste of a good fire.'

Kate laughed, sitting down next to him. She

was not quite touching him, but somehow it felt as if she were. 'Fred made a good job of it.'

'Yes, he did. If he built it.'

'I don't imagine Edie did.'

'No, I don't imagine she did either. When I was a teenager, it was considered good form to collect up a few sticks and build a new fire when you left. Then, when you came back, someone else's fire would be there and you just lit it.'

'Ah. So there's no need to search around for something to burn while your girlfriend's sitting on a rock and shivering.' Kate grinned at him.

'That might be a consideration.' He stretched, holding his hands out to the warmth of the blaze. 'So. You're going to say yes, are you?'

He was teasing her, that was obvious. And if Kate denied it then it would only appear that she was protesting too much.

'I might. As Fred says, a doctor's a very good catch.'

Ethan chuckled. 'Long hours? Evenings on your own?'

'Never out of a job. Good pay scales.' Kate grinned up at him. 'I think Fred had an eye on the practical.'

'Having the time to be with someone *is* practical.'

There was a sudden catch in his voice. Ethan leaned forward, poking the fire with a stick so that it burned brightly, suddenly lost in his own thoughts, which seemed to be dancing among the flames.

'You seem very sure of that.'

He turned down the corners of his mouth. 'I am. I was working pretty hard when Jenna died. We'd just bought the house and she'd given up work when Sam was born. I wasn't around very much.'

Kate could see why that would matter to him, but it was something that a lot of people did. Buying houses, having kids. It all cost money. She wondered whether that was really the right thing to say to Ethan, and decided that this was one of those situations where there was no right thing to say. You just had to do your best.

'You were providing for your family.'

'Yeah, that's how we both looked at it. Jenna had been under the weather for a few days with a urinary infection. I'd given her a prescription for some antibiotics, and she said she was feeling better, so I went to work. I worked late that evening, and spent the night at the hospital. I called her and she said that she was okay.'

I'm okay. The very thing that she had said to Ethan. No wonder he'd refused to take her word for it, and had kept nagging away at her until she was honest with him. Kate swallowed hard. 'But she wasn't.'

'No. The infection spread to her kidney and she was sick…couldn't keep the antibiotics down. Then it got into her bloodstream and she developed sepsis. I got the call the following afternoon. My mother had gone over there to help her out with Sam and had called an ambulance.'

'But it was too late.' Kate knew that sepsis could kill quickly. The body's reaction to infection, it caused the vital organs to shut down, and once that happened it was difficult to reverse.

'Yes. She died two days later.'

'I'm so sorry, Ethan.'

He shook his head, staring into the fire. 'I've learned to live with it. But you see, a doctor who isn't around when his family needs him isn't as good a catch as Fred thinks.'

He blamed himself. 'But you can't think…'

'I don't think, I *know.* I wasn't there.'

'But…' This was crazy. No one could be there for someone all the time. And if Ethan was responsible, then so was his wife. Kate pressed her lips together. Maybe she shouldn't say that.

'But what?'

'I just think you can't be there for someone twenty-four hours a day. I tried to lock myself away from harm once, and it didn't work.'

'That's what you think—that it's like trying to lock them away from harm?'

Maybe she'd said too much. But Kate believed it, and she couldn't take it back now. 'Yes, it is.'

'Yeah, it's what I think too.' There was a note of resignation in his voice.

'But you don't feel it?'

'No, I don't.'

And no one could help him with that. Kate supposed that she wasn't the first person who'd told him that his wife's death wasn't his fault, and she probably wouldn't be the last. He'd grieved, and learned to move forward with his life. But he just couldn't get rid of the guilt.

'I really wish I had chocolate.' Kate puffed out a breath and heard Ethan chuckle quietly.

'What, you came out without chocolate? That was very remiss of you. Think you'll make it back?'

'Not for me, for you. It's a coping mechanism.'

'My coping mechanisms are just fine. But thank you for your concern.'

Kate shot him a look of disbelief but said nothing. Ethan had thought his coping mechanisms were working perfectly until he'd met Kate. He'd accepted that he was responsible for what had happened to Jenna and that what he needed to do from now on was to concentrate on taking care of Sam. That would be very easy if you removed Kate from the mix.

But he couldn't wish her away. He wouldn't do that, even if he knew that he was quite capable of failing her. He could call it selfish, or he could call it listening to what Kate had said and believing her.

Here, with Kate sitting so close, believing her seemed like a possibility. When he turned to look at her she was gazing at him, wide-eyed, hair the colour of the flames in front of them and just as unruly.

He stretched out his arm, putting it around her shoulders, and Kate nestled closer. They sat for a long time, watching the fire together, and then finally Ethan reached up, his fingers brushing her cheek.

If he took it slow, then she'd have the chance to stop him at any time. But then Kate preempted that by stretching up and planting a kiss on the side of his mouth.

So soft, so very sweet, yet with all the promise of something that might break the both of them if they gave in to it. Ethan wasn't someone who usually courted danger, but now the risk heightened the pleasure.

His hand moved to the back of her head and he did what he'd been wanting to do for a long time. He kissed her properly.

* * *

As soon as her lips touched his, Kate knew that this was a risk. But, despite all that, she wanted him to kiss her more than she wanted to breathe.

When he did, it was a wild voyage, discovering a forgotten pleasure. Finding that she'd been wrong when she'd thought that one kiss couldn't possibly send shimmers racing through her body, making her fingers tremble and her toes curl. It was breathless, heart-pounding, joy.

'I've been thinking about doing that for a while.' He whispered the words close to her ear, although even if he'd screamed them no one would have heard. Kate bunched the front of his jacket tight in her fingers.

'Tell me you're not planning on making me wait so long for the next one….'

His lips grazed her cheek, sending shivers through her. Maybe this was how it would be if he made love to her. Taking her right to the point of no return, and then slowing, just so that they could both feel the need.

She stretched up, kissing him, and felt Ethan's arm around her waist, pulling her onto his lap. He kissed her again, demanding this time, and she felt desire begin to pulse deep inside.

No… Too much. Too soon. Mind over matter was one thing, but she hadn't expected this.

Kate drew back, pushing the feeling down before she lost control.

She could see it in his eyes too. The shocked acknowledgement that this wasn't just a kiss. Which was a problem, because Kate could barely handle just kissing him.

'I'm sorry, Kate.'

'It's all right. I started it.'

'We both started it, together. And perhaps we both have to end it now.' Ethan shrugged. 'I can't. I don't think of myself as having the right to do this.'

His guilt again. He'd grieved for his wife, and let that go, but he couldn't let go of the guilt. Ethan's world had somehow become smaller, leaving no room for him to move beyond just he and Sam.

'Maybe I'm not ready for it either.' These were stolen moments, only possible because tonight Sam happened to be with his grandparents. Kate needed someone to be there on a rather more permanent basis than that.

They were silent for a long time, both staring at the fire. That wasn't going to do any good. There weren't any answers there.

'The fire's burning down. We should go.'

'Yeah.' He got to his feet, helping her up, and then kicking at the fire to extinguish it. 'Perhaps we won't worry about rebuilding it.'

'No, we must. I can't break with tradition, not on my first time here.' She smiled awkwardly up at him.

Suddenly it was possible to think that they could be just friends who had stumbled over the line by mistake in the darkness. They found bracken and twigs for the new fire, and Ethan built it while Kate watched.

'That'll do, I think.'

'Yes. It'll do very nicely.' Maybe the next couple who came up here and put a match to the fire that Ethan had left for them would have better luck and not discover that it had all been a mistake.

Kate took one last look around to make sure that they hadn't left anything behind and then followed Ethan out of the cave and onto the wide causeway for the long walk back to his car.

CHAPTER TWELVE

NEITHER OF THEM had spoken much on their way back to Ethan's car and he hadn't heard from Kate the next day. That was probably for the best. He needed some distance, to get back into the routine of friendship, and he guessed that Kate did too.

All the same, he missed her. The slow meander of Sunday and the morning rush of Monday did nothing to erode the memory of how she'd kissed him. Even the careful, concentrated work of the day couldn't drive her completely from his thoughts.

He knew that going to see Edie before he left the hospital for the evening might involve bumping into Kate. But Ethan took the risk and the sudden thump in his chest when he saw her sitting at Edie's bedside told him that he couldn't just turn around and walk away. Watching from the entrance doors of the ward, he saw the two women carefully unpacking a cloth bag that Kate had laid on the bed. A packet of face wipes, some chocolate and some fruit. Small gifts, each one of which made Edie smile.

'Oh! Lavender water. Thank you, dear!' Ethan heard Edie's exclamation, and saw Kate reach forward, opening the bottle for Edie and tipping it so that she could dab a little onto Edie's wrist.

'Behind your ears?'

'Oh, yes, please. How thoughtful.'

It was thoughtful. A little luxury to chase away the smell of antiseptic. Ethan approached Edie's bed.

Kate jumped when she saw him and the thought that his presence was responsible for the sudden reddening of her cheeks sent a tingle down Ethan's spine. He shot Kate a smile and then turned his attention to Edie.

'How are you?'

'Much better, thank you. I've been a lot of trouble, haven't I? To a lot of people.' Edie twisted down the corners of her mouth.

'No one thinks that.' Kate patted Edie's hand. 'Everyone just wanted you to be safe and we're glad that you are.'

'I've made a decision.' Edie gave a firm little nod. 'My son found a really nice flat in a sheltered housing complex for us, but I said that I could manage Fred. I think it's time, though. We need a bit of help. And I'd be able to have a nurse in to look after him while I go out with my friends once in a while.'

'Where is Fred now?' Ethan knew that hospital was challenging for people with dementia and wondered if there was anything he could do to help.

'He's at home. My daughter's staying with him while I'm here.' Edie smiled, leaning towards Kate. 'Actually, it's rather nice. A bit of a rest.'

'Well, you'll have more help when you move into the sheltered accommodation.' Kate gave a little frown, obviously not sure how Edie might feel about having to move.

'Yes, I will. I'm rather looking forward to it, actually.'

'Nice lady.' Ethan held the door of the ward open for Kate.

'Yes. I hope she'll be all right. It's a big step, moving into sheltered accommodation.'

'I don't see what else she can do. She can't manage Fred on her own any more.'

Kate nodded. 'That's clear enough. And I suppose that life will be much easier for her, once she has help to look after Fred properly. It's a big change for her, though.'

'Life's full of changes. We have to make them into new beginnings.' When he looked at Kate,

Ethan had the courage to say it. Almost the faith to believe it.

'Yes. I hope Edie's new beginning is a good one.'

'She seems to think it will be.' The touch of Kate's lips echoed through his memory, leaving him trembling.

The thought that he'd decided never to love anyone again suddenly made him feel like a traitor. As if he'd turned his back on all the people who'd taught him how to love, telling them that love meant nothing.

'Would you like to go for coffee—something to eat, maybe?' Kate could be depended on to want something to eat.

'I'd like to, but…' She twisted her mouth in an expression of regret. 'I've got to get back to the surgery. I'm working this evening.'

'Too bad. Another time, maybe.'

She thought about it for a moment. 'How about the weekend? I'm pretty busy this week, as one of the other vets at the practice is on holiday and so everyone's filling in for her. It would be nice to do it some time when I don't have to rush away.'

Ethan smiled. Kate wanted to take time with him. He wanted that too. 'Why don't you come over on Friday evening and I'll cook? Sam's going over to my parents'. He and my dad have a project they're working on together. So I can cook something a bit different.'

The menu wasn't really the issue. Maybe being alone with him would be, but Kate only hesitated for a moment.

'So we won't be having bangers and mash?'

'I was thinking maybe not.'

'Hmm. Shame. What time shall I come?'

One of the disadvantages of knowing Ethan was that Kate had become obsessed by her own wardrobe. It was no longer something that just got opened once or twice a day, for long enough to pull out something which more or less matched and was appropriate for the weather. It had to be sorted through and studied carefully.

She puffed out a breath. She'd taken three perfectly good summer dresses out and hung them over the tops of the doors. One would be just as good as the other.

She held the red one up against her, looking in the mirror. A bit short. She didn't want to look as if she was trying to seduce him. When she did the same with the green one, it was a bit long. Kate made a face at herself.

'They're just knees, for goodness' sakes. He's seen lots of different knees before. He's a doctor.'

Kate puffed out another breath. The dark-blue

one. It fell just above the knee, slimline and a wrap-around at the front. Before she could change her mind again, she put the other two dresses back into the wardrobe and banged the door shut. Her car was playing up and she had decided that, rather than have it conk out on her again, it was best to take it straight to the garage. If she was going to wash her hair and blow dry it into something approximating a style before the taxi arrived to take her to Ethan's house, then she'd better get moving.

Ethan had thought carefully about the menu for that evening. A couple of free-range steaks, done with peppercorn sauce and a salad. Nothing too fancy, but at least he could indulge his penchant for a medium-rare steak without Sam wrinkling his nose and telling him that his dinner was bleeding.

He made the salad and scrubbed some potatoes, taking the meat out of the fridge so that it went into the pan at room temperature. Then he set up the table in the conservatory, laying it carefully. A couple of candles didn't seem too far over the top.

Kate arrived at eight, blowing every rational thought from his head. She stood on the doorstep, wearing a blue dress, her hair tamed into a mass of curls at the back of her head. Ethan felt as if he was a teenager on a first date.

'Can I come in?' She was clearly unwilling to squeeze past him as he stood motionless, blocking the doorway.

'Uh…yes, of course.' Ethan remembered his manners and showed her through to the conservatory. A bottle of wine stood ready, and he poured a glass for her and a glass of sparkling water for himself.

He shooed her from the kitchen when she tried to help with cooking the steaks, reckoning that a steady hand was probably wise when dealing with a hot pan. He served the dinner, eating almost nothing in favour of watching her. It seemed that Kate, too, was on her best behaviour.

But dessert changed all that. When he set the two glass dishes on the table, she let out a little scream.

'Ethan!'

'I made it myself.'

'Home-made tiramisu! We can't possibly eat this here.' An impish smile spread across her face.

'Where do you want to eat it?' He followed the direction of her pointing spoon, and smiled. 'Good idea.'

He opened the doors of the conservatory,

picking up a rug from one of the chairs and spreading it on the lawn, at the place where the lights from the house met the dark shadows at the end of the garden. Kate almost danced after him, holding the two dishes.

'So, you're not one of those doctors who gives a girl a hard time over dessert.' She plonked herself down on the rug, tucking her bare legs underneath her. The front of her dress gaped a little, giving him a view of one more delicious inch of flesh above her knee.

'Actually, I might be. Tonight I'll make an exception.'

She laughed, leaning towards him. 'Three-point-four.'

'Three-point-four, what?'

'My cholesterol level. Three-point-four.'

'Not bad.' Ethan chuckled at her outraged look. 'All right, then, it's pretty good. That's not all there is to it, though. But there's nothing wrong with something sweet from time to time, as long as you don't overdo it.'

She giggled, and Ethan's heart began to thump in his chest. Surely he could believe his own judgement. A little of Kate's sweetness…?

Ethan had ignored all her protests and insisted on driving her home. Kate hurried up her front path, aware that Ethan was watching her from his car, and waved to him before closing the front door. This evening had been lovely and she hadn't wanted it to end.

But all good things did come to an end. Maybe that was what made them good, leaving while you still wanted more and before the inevitable disappointment of real life set in. She automatically walked to the back door, hardly looking at it before she turned away to make her way upstairs, still lost in the dream that centred around Ethan.

The doorbell rang with pause between the 'ding' and the 'dong' as if someone had kept their finger on the bell for a little too long. Kate walked back downstairs, taking her phone from her bag as she went and stood in the hallway, staring at the front door.

'It's Ethan.'

His voice sounded muffled by the wooden barrier between them.

'Oh! What…what do you want?' She knew exactly what he wanted. Or rather she *hoped* she knew.

Kate opened the door and found him leaning against the entrance to the porch.

'I'd really like to come in.' His eyes were dark, his blond hair highlighted by the light from the hallway.

'I'd really like you to come in.'

For a moment they both hesitated and then Ethan stepped over the threshold, closing the door behind him. One of his hands drifted to her waist, his fingers brushing the fabric of her dress, and Kate felt her heart thump in her chest.

'Ethan, I... You know I get frightened at night sometimes. That's not why I want you here and—'

He put his finger across her lips. 'And I get lonely. That's not why I want to be here with you.'

'Why *do* you want to be here?'

He pulled her close in a sudden, powerful movement that left no room for doubt. Ethan wanted her and she wanted him back.

Kate pushed him back against the door in her eagerness to kiss him. Felt his chest move in a low sigh which sounded like the sudden release of everything that had kept them apart.

They were both trembling, with arousal and...something else that wasn't quite fear and wasn't quite shyness. It was the hesitancy of having been wounded. But Ethan's hands, his lips, gave her courage. Everything around them began to blur, leaving only him in sharp focus.

She broke away from him, backing towards the stairs, her finger crooked in an invitation to follow. 'Come upstairs...'

He moved fast, but not fast enough. Kate

eluded his outstretched hand and ran up the stairs. He caught her at the top, backing her towards the bathroom.

'Wrong way.'

He grinned as Kate pulled him towards the bedroom door.

It seemed as if it were another lifetime when she'd last had a man in her bedroom. But, when Kate suddenly didn't know what to do, Ethan did. When he pulled his shirt over his head, the need to see and touch washed everything else away.

'You are beautiful.' He was broad-shouldered, skin the colour of honey. He was a perfect man, made even more perfect by the touch of the sun and hard physical work. She felt soft skin and the flex of muscle when she ran her fingers across his chest.

Ethan wrapped his arms around her, loosening the pins which held her hair back from her face. 'You have gorgeous hair…wonderful lips and…'

He tugged gently at the zip on the back of her dress. When Kate kissed him, he slowly drew it down. He made her *feel* beautiful—undressing her slowly, whispering his appreciation for every part of her body.

It would only take one more step—a few more scraps of clothing and then the delicious slide of his skin against hers. But it wasn't easy to take that step, for either of them. There was too much fear and too much pain. Too much wanting to be free of it and not knowing if they could.

Kate reached up, caressing his cheek. 'I can't think of one thing that could happen between us tonight that wouldn't be okay.'

'So you have no expectations? A guy could feel hurt.'

'I have expectations. I just want you to know that you tip my world upside down. And, if I falter, then it's not because anything's wrong. I'm just feeling my way.'

'Which makes us free. We can be whatever we want to be.' He brushed his lips against the lobe of her ear.

He understood. That was all she needed. She kissed him, her fingers touching his cheek, and he groaned, his body growing harder.

'I love the way I turn you on.' The thought that just her touch could arouse him so much make Kate's head spin.

'I'm not always this easy.' He chuckled, nipping the lobe of her ear.

'Just with me?'

'Seems that way.'

'I like that even better…' She caught her breath as he lifted her up, laying her down on the bed.

* * *

It occurred to Ethan, during the brief moments when he could think at all, that this dizzy, heady reaction was just the result of an instinctive craving to feel the touch of someone's skin against his. But he knew it wasn't. Only Kate could have made him turn his car around and do the unthinkable.

He'd thought that learning to love was a one-time thing. Done, then broken and now forgotten. But with Kate he knew that he could learn again.

And tonight was all about Kate, only about her—the way she moved, the light in her eyes and the softness of her skin. And, more than that, it was about her gentle nature—the way she made him feel that there was no fixed outcome for tonight, just a sweet exploration of possibilities.

They made love, staring into each other's eyes, feeling the warmth grow into an intoxicating heat. When she came it seemed almost as if it had taken her by surprise, something that hadn't been sought or worked for, but an expression of how she felt at that moment.

He felt a bead of sweat trickle down his back. One moment, just enough to kiss her as he felt the pulse of her body weaken again. Then feeling robbed him of any thought, other than the knowledge that when he cried out he called her name.

They clung together for a long time and then she moved away from him, curling up on her side of the bed, watching. When Ethan reached out to her, she twined her fingers through his.

Her brilliant smile told him all he needed to know. Drawing her close, he folded his arms around her.

CHAPTER THIRTEEN

AT SOME POINT all the uncertainty had gone. How much Ethan was willing to give, and what he wanted to keep. When they'd curled up together, after that first time, it had been clear that he was ready to give everything.

'Favourite…food.' They'd already covered films, books and places, and now Ethan's lips twitched into a knowing smile.

'You heard my stomach rumble?'

'No. But, since you always seem to be hungry, it's a question that interests me.'

Kate thought for a moment. 'At the moment… Something cold.'

'Ice cream. Have you got any?'

She jabbed her finger against his shoulder. 'Do I have ice cream? I just made love with you. Don't make me think you don't know me at all.'

'I thought you might have eaten it all.' He laughed, pulling her close for a kiss. 'How many flavours?'

'Three.'

'Chocolate.' He brushed his lips against hers, and she felt a tingle run up her spine. This was actually far better than chocolate ice cream. 'Caramel?'

'You do know me, then.' It felt as if Ethan knew her better than anyone. 'Care to take a guess at the other one?'

'Passion fruit?' His innocent blue eyes suddenly turned wicked, and Kate felt his hand slide down her back. This was a new Ethan. One who didn't hesitate, but who trusted himself enough to take what he wanted. That was a good thought.

'No passion fruit. I have strawberry, though.'

'Just as good.'

He made it better than Kate could ever have imagined. A cold spoon trailed across her skin. Ethan's lips made her shiver and melt, all at the same time, and when he rolled her onto her side, running his tongue down her spine, she gasped.

'You like that?'

No need to answer. Kate felt him brush her hair forward, over one shoulder, exposing the back of her neck. Then his arms slid around her, one around her waist, the other hand cupping her breast. Heat engulfed her and she relaxed in his arms as he kissed the back of her neck.

'Not fair...' She wanted him to feel this trembling desire too.

'What isn't fair?'

'I can't touch you...' Her hands groped for something to hold on to and found only a pillow to grab. His hands moved, caressing her, and another jolt of pleasure made Kate squirm.

'And when you do?'

'I'll pay you back, Ethan.'

'Oh, yes? How, exactly?' He rolled her onto her back, covering her body with his. 'I want all the details.'

He loved this as much as she did. This long, slow burn, which turned the ache of wanting him into drawn-out pleasure. It ebbed and flowed between them, whispers and kisses, caresses. When finally Kate pushed him down onto the bed, reaching for the condoms on the bedside table, her shaking fingers fumbled with the foil packet and he took it from her.

He pulled her on top of him, a sharp sigh escaping his lips. 'Let me look at you. Just for a moment.'

His clear-eyed gaze said the words before he could speak. 'You're so beautiful, Kate.'

She believed it. Somehow making do with a glance in the mirror had slipped away, and she knew that in Ethan's eyes she *was* beautiful. And she trusted Ethan.

'And you are...perfect.' She ran her fingers across his chest. 'Just perfect.'

He moved beneath her and the slow burn began to turn into a fever. He *was* just perfect.

Well-made beds were over-rated. Cushions and pillows in complementary colours piled at the head were just an unnecessary complication and had found their way unheeded onto the floor. Just two crumpled sheets mapped out the course of their love-making last night and they were more than enough to make Ethan smile this morning.

He disentangled his foot from the corner of the sheet that covered them. *Almost* covered them. Kate looked like a Botticelli angel, white fabric draped around her body, her arms and legs bare. Ethan leaned over and kissed her, and she opened her eyes.

'Sorry to wake you this early. But I've got to go.'

She nodded sleepily. 'Sam?'

'Yes. It's a thing we have—breakfast.'

'It's a good thing. Go.'

He wished that he could have a breakfast thing with Kate as well. That he could stay here, raid her kitchen and make more than she could eat. It was a challenge, but one he would be more than willing to take on.

But, however hard he tried, he couldn't be in two places at once.

'Go.' Kate had seen his hesitation and was smiling. 'Here, take this with you.'

She pressed a kiss onto his lips and all the warmth of last night, everything they'd made together, flooded back into his senses. He felt her gaze follow him as he got out of bed, and gathered his clothes up from the floor. Instinctively his pace slowed a little.

'Watching you get dressed is almost as good as watching you get undressed.' Kate was propped up on her elbow, grinning broadly.

'Care to give me a hand?' One of the buttons of his shirt had been almost wrenched from its moorings, after he'd tugged impatiently at it last night. Even that small detail of a memory made him smile.

'No. I'm fine right here.'

She was better than fine. Sleepy-eyed and still half-wrapped in the sheet, she was gorgeous. Only one thing could stop him from tearing his clothes off and making love to her again.

'Stay right there. I'll call you later.' He bent over, planting his hands on the mattress on either side of her body.

'Video call?'

He grinned suddenly. 'In that case, I'll call earlier.'

She stretched lazily. ‘Don’t rush. I think I’ll have a lie-in this morning.’

Ethan chuckled, dipping to kiss her forehead. He was already mentally counting the minutes that it would take to go home, shower, then get to his parents’ house and make breakfast for Sam. Then find a secluded spot in the garden to make his call.

‘Where’s your phone?’

‘Downstairs, I think. I took it with me when I went to answer the door.’

Ethan found her phone on the hall table, switching it on briefly to check it was charged. Then he brought it upstairs and put it down on the empty pillow next to her. One last kiss and then he tore himself away from her.

Kate’s phone rang sooner than she’d expected. She jabbed at the ‘answer’ icon, wishing she’d thought to get out of bed and untangle some of the knots in her hair.

He was sitting in the morning sunlight, a neat garden in the background, grinning. ‘Hey there, beautiful.’

Kate ran her hand across her unruly curls and he chuckled.

‘Don’t! I’ve only just woken up again.’

‘I can see that. It really suits you.’

She raised her eyebrows. 'What, my hair all over the place?'

'Especially that.' The slight quirk of his lips told Kate exactly what he was thinking. To be honest, she was thinking the same right now. But last night was…last night. Neither of them had said anything about this morning, and it was uncharted territory.

'You got back in time for Sam?' Kate decided to play it safe.

'Yes. He's eating toast with my dad at the moment. They're discussing their project.'

'What on earth is the project?' Whatever it was it seemed to be taking a bit of time and energy. This was the second Saturday running that Sam had stayed at his grandparents'.

'They're making a space station for superheroes. It's in the field at the end of the garden.'

'Really? How big is it, then?'

'It's about the size of my conservatory, only the roof's not quite so high. Apparently, I'm surplus to requirements at this stage, but I might be needed later for some of the heavy work.'

Kate chuckled. 'Too bad.'

'Yeah. A year ago he thought I knew everything about everything. Now there are a whole range of things I don't know about.'

'Do you mind?' Kate settled back against the pillows. This was nice, warm and friendly, a different strand of intimacy from the one they'd had last night.

Ethan shrugged. 'Yeah, I mind. I'm trying not to, though, because I wouldn't have it any other way.'

He fell silent for a moment, his gaze fixed on her. If he asked her to lose the sheet that was currently wrapped tight around her, she'd do it in a heartbeat. But that would be less, somehow. It would break this new bond that was forming between them.

'So, what are you doing today?' Ethan seemed to understand that too, and his question made Kate smile. It had been a long time since anyone had been much interested in what she did on her days off.

'The usual. Shopping. Washing and ironing…' Maybe she'd leave the washing until tomorrow. One more night spent surrounded by Ethan's scent.

'You said that this weekend might be okay for us to pick up Sam's puppy.' There was a sudden tension in his voice. Kate had conveniently forgotten all about that, too afraid to suggest seeing Ethan again this weekend.

'Yes, I did. If you're ready to do that, then perhaps we could go over there tomorrow afternoon.'

Ethan nodded. 'I was thinking, if you'd like to

come over tomorrow and have lunch with Sam and me, then we could go and fetch the puppy afterwards.'

Sunday lunch. It was a brave new inroad into territory that Kate had promised herself she wouldn't think about. Particularly not with Ethan.

'Yes. That sounds great, I'd love to. What time?'

He grinned. 'Any time after six am?'

'I'll come at twelve. Don't want to surprise you both in your racing car pyjamas' If Ethan wore pyjamas, Kate would eat the sheet she was currently wrapped in.

'Racing cars are so last year. He's got Ambigulon pyjamas now.'

'Ambigulon?'

'Yeah. Superhero stuff. Ambigulon has a glowing amber crystal which shoots power rays. They either heal a person or hurt them, depending on whether they have a pure heart.'

'Blimey! That's complicated.'

Ethan rolled his eyes. 'Trust me, it's just the tip of the iceberg. Superheroes are *very* complicated...'

Talking to Kate had been very complicated. However much Ethan wanted to tell himself that this was just two friends who happened to find each other attractive, it had been impossible to maintain the pretence. He'd found himself sharing his thoughts and feelings with her. The stories about Sam that he'd so often wished he could share with someone.

Ethan had told himself that asking her to lunch was a very obvious next step. Treating her as a friend. But everything he did seemed only to deepen the one role that he still wasn't sure he was capable of. A lover. Someone who protected and nurtured.

When the doorbell rang at exactly midday, Sam ran to meet Kate, aiming his Ambigulon crystal at the door, which stayed resolutely in place. Ethan herded him out of the way, getting rid of the obstruction in a more conventional manner.

'Hi. Am I too early?' Kate was standing on the doorstep, looking delicious. Ethan wondered whether, in common with Ambigulon's crystal, she had the power to divine whether a man's heart was pure or not. And what the outcome would be if his was put to the test.

'You're right on time. I'm running a little late. Sam, show Kate into the conservatory and I'll get on with lunch.' He flashed her a grin and she rewarded him with a brilliant smile.

Through the open door of the kitchen, Ethan could hear Sam chivvying her through into the conservatory and instructing her to sit down in a chair that he'd selected for her.

'Are we going to get the puppy now?' Sam reiterated the question that he'd been asking Ethan all morning, obviously keen on getting a second opinion.

'Not yet. After lunch.' Kate's voice was full of laughter and tenderness. 'Have you thought of a name for him yet?'

Ethan grinned down at the roast potatoes in the pan in front of him, wondering what she'd make of the answer.

'Sam. I'm calling him Sam.'

'Sam? But that's your name.' The rustle of skirts and the faint creak of wicker as Kate moved in her seat. The sounds were almost unbearably erotic.

'How are you going to know whether your dad is calling to you or the puppy?' A short pause and then Kate laughed. 'Is that the point of calling him Sam—so you can pretend that you thought Dad was calling the puppy and not you?'

Sam sounded as if he was jumping up and down, laughing. 'Yessss!'

'Oh. So the puppy's going to get to eat all your ice cream?'

Ethan closed his eyes, silently begging Kate not to mention ice cream while he was in the room. He wasn't sure how long it would be before he could look at another tub of strawberry ice cream without thinking of last night.

'And is he going to wear your T-shirt?'

Silence. Sam was obviously thinking about the ramifications of his choice of names.

'Or… I can call him Ambigulon.'

Ethan shook his head. The idea of shouting, 'Ambigulon!' at the top of his voice to call the puppy back to heel didn't exactly appeal to him.

'That's a good name. But wouldn't it be a bit inconvenient if the puppy could reverse gravity?'

Ethan was sure he hadn't mentioned reversing gravity to Kate. The idea that she'd done her research on topics that would interest Sam was a novel one. She was clearly making an effort with him.

'I think… Arthur!'

Where had Sam got that from? It wasn't a family name and, as far as Ethan knew, it wasn't the name of anyone that Sam knew. But, actually, he could get used to Arthur.

'What does your dad think?'

Ethan decided to intervene. Popping his head out through the kitchen door, he saw Kate seated on the edge of one of the wicker chairs. Sam was leaning against her legs, smoothing the hem of her blue-and-white-striped summer dress with one hand. It was a curious reversal of roles. When Sam was around Ethan didn't get to touch her, but his son had none of those inhibitions.

'I think that Arthur's a very good name.' He mouthed a 'thank you' in Kate's direction and she flashed him a grin.

'So do I.' She smiled gravely down at Sam.

'Okay. Arthur.' Sam nodded, as if the matter was now closed. 'When are we going to get him?'

'After lunch.' Ethan found himself chorusing the words with Kate, and she looked up at him, blushing. Ethan chuckled, turning back to the kitchen.

Lunch was an exercise in Sam trying to eat as fast as he could and Ethan trying to slow him down. When the boy wriggled down from his seat, obviously ready to go, Ethan shot her a look of apology.

'Shall we have coffee when we get back?' She smiled at him, casually pushing her hand across the table towards Ethan, wondering whether he might respond.

'If you don't mind. I think he might burst if we make him wait any longer.'

Sam ran out of the conservatory and into the house and suddenly she felt Ethan's fingers around hers. As he raised them to his lips, his eyes seemed to flash a brighter blue.

'I don't want you to make any mistake over my intentions, Kate.'

She felt her cheeks redden. All her resolutions that needing Ethan in the heat of the night didn't mean she couldn't be independent the following morning seemed a little stupid right now. She needed him, but she didn't really know whether he even wanted her for more than a brief fling.

'We didn't have any intentions, did we?'

'I do now. If I ask whether we can take things slowly, one step at a time, then please don't think I'm not serious about wanting to make things work between us.'

Making things work. She wanted to make things work more than anything and she knew that both of them needed a little time to get used to the idea of doing that. 'Slow is good. I'd like to take things slowly too.'

'Slow it is, then.' His lips curved into the same smile that he'd had on his lips last night, when taking it slowly had been an exercise in everything that was delicious. He rose from his seat, bending to kiss her cheek before Sam scooted back into the room, dropping Ethan's car keys into his hand.

The afternoon was turning into the kind of sunny Sunday afternoon that seemed to have been lost irretrievably in Kate's childhood, when she'd felt that she could run barefoot in the grass, her dress swishing around her legs, without any danger of cutting her feet. When the sun couldn't burn her and she couldn't get wet in a sudden shower of rain. Where the only thing that could touch her was the look on Sam's face as he hugged his new puppy, the blue of Ethan's eyes and the sure feeling that whatever happened next couldn't disappoint her.

Sam seemed to know instinctively that Arthur was small and frightened. He coaxed him gently from the animal carrier, helping him to explore his new world. After an afternoon of exploring, the two of them wore each other out at much the same time, curling up in one of the wicker chairs in the conservatory together and falling asleep.

Ethan had turned the chair slightly, so that its high back obscured Sam's view of the conservatory steps where he and Kate sat.

'No regrets?' Kate knew that he must have mixed feelings about this. Sam was growing up and beginning to be independent of him. And Ethan must still think about Jeff.

'None. Sam wanted this.'

'And you?'

'I'm…ready to move on too.' His tone was soft, but there was a finality about it. As if he'd thought about this and come to a conclusion. 'Did you see Sam's face when Arthur started playing with his dog toys?'

'It would have been difficult to miss.' Kate laughed quietly. 'Thank you for letting me be a part of it all.'

His arm was behind her. Not quite around her, but a tentative signal that it might be if she wanted it. Kate moved a little closer to him, and Ethan put his arm properly around her shoulders. That was better.

'Thank you for being here. And for making this afternoon happen.' He brushed a kiss against her hair. 'And for talking him out of calling the puppy Ambigulon.'

'That wasn't so difficult.'

'Sam can be very stubborn when he wants to be.' Ethan grinned.

'And you're not stubborn at all.' Kate smirked at him.

'Not even slightly. I'm always open to reason.'

'Of course you are.' Kate turned and kissed him. He responded, pulling her tight against him. He was definitely open to that.

But even if Sam was sleeping, and wouldn't have been able to see them even if he woke, he was still there. Maybe that was a good thing. The loud voice which told her that everything was all right had got the upper hand this afternoon. But the doubts, the fear of losing herself and finding that he would let her down, were all still there.

'I'm sorry that…' He shrugged. 'Sam.'

'I know. It's okay. You have to put him first, always. I wouldn't like you very much if you didn't.'

He nodded. 'I wouldn't like myself very much. But there are times when I wish I could take the rest of the evening off. Right now, I do.'

'Another time.'

'Yes. I'd love that.'

He leaned over and kissed her. Warmly but with an echo of all that Ethan could do to her. It was enough, for now.

CHAPTER FOURTEEN

YOU WERE SUPPOSED to look forward to Saturday night, weren't you? Kate couldn't remember having looked forward to one with such trembling anticipation before. Ethan called, saying that Sam would be staying with his grandparents again on Saturday. This time there was no pretence about happening to be alone and wanting some company. He asked her whether she might like to come out with him on a date.

Ethan took nothing for granted, his tone a little halting and formal. Kate accepted his invitation and she heard him laugh quietly.

'I'm glad you said yes.'

'I'm glad you called to ask.' She was grinning at the phone, wondering if he felt sixteen as well—that nervous thrill that accompanied a first date.

'Well, I have to go, now. I need to pop out into the garden for a moment and run round in circles, punching the air.'

Kate laughed. Even though they were both a little older and much wiser somehow, they'd both managed to put the intervening years aside and go back to the beginning. Could they really be sixteen again, unlearn everything they knew and start over?

'I have to go upstairs and fling my wardrobe doors open. Scream that I have nothing to wear...'

'What are you wearing now?' Ethan's tone took on a note of the hunger that she felt for him.

'Blue jeans. A red shirt.'

'You look beautiful. Come exactly as you are.'

Kate did just that, although she'd added a pair of high, strappy sandals and some jewellery which had taken her almost as long to decide on as selecting her whole outfit. When she answered the door to him, his face broke into a broad grin.

'You look far more gorgeous than I've been imagining you might. And that's a tough proposition.' He held out his arm and Kate felt herself thrill at the slightly stiff, old-fashioned gesture. Last weekend hadn't just been something that adults had done and then moved on from because it was much too complicated to contemplate anything else. Ethan had come a-courting. There was no mistaking it.

She stepped outside, locking the front door

behind her, and took his arm. The two of them couldn't quite fit on the narrow front path and Ethan walked to one side on the grass.

'This is nice.' She smiled up at him as he opened the gate for her.

'I'm a little rusty. I haven't done this in a while.'

'If this is you being a little rusty, I can't wait to see what happens when you really get into your stride.' The thought was both exciting and terrifying. But Ethan was doing all the right things to calm her fears. Taking it slowly. Taking it tenderly.

'Thank you, ma'am. I'll do my best not to disappoint.'

He couldn't have disappointed her if he'd tried. She loved the way he'd drawn her hand up to his lips, looking into her eyes when he kissed her fingertips. She loved the quiet, country pub where the food was good and they could eat outside. Loved the way he was so interested in hearing about the things in her life—her job, her family, her childhood—and the way he told her about his.

'Come back with me.' He'd paid the bill and they were still sitting at their table, the lights around them beginning to glow bright in the gathering darkness.

'For coffee?' Ethan's smile told her that if it *was* just for coffee that would be fine with him.

'No. Not for coffee.' She leaned across the table towards him. 'Or don't you do that kind of thing on a first date?'

This was crazy. They'd already done *that kind of thing.* But Ethan understood. Last week had been one of those sweet things that had been unplanned, done to escape from the real world. Tonight *was* the real world and if they spent it together then it was a new and different hope for the future.

'There's nothing I'd like to do more...'

They made love by flickering candlelight, the open windows in her bedroom allowing what breeze there was in the still evening to caress their bodies. And, for every moment of it, Ethan was there with her. In the long, tender embraces when it felt as if he was making love to every inch of her. In the strong, passionate climaxes which came again and again, finally leaving them still, tangled together on the bed.

'Would you like some wine?' Kate stretched luxuriantly on the crumpled sheets. The bottle of wine and the ice-bucket had been ready in the kitchen and she'd fetched them on their way upstairs. She was glad now she'd remembered. Kate didn't want to be away from Ethan for even a moment.

'So...you had this all planned.' He reached for the corkscrew, his gaze flipping to the two glasses that sat on the bedside table.

'Yes, I did. Only, you didn't keep to the plan.'

He raised his eyebrows, taking the bottle from the half-melted ice and holding it to one side as he pulled the cork so that water didn't drip all over the bed. 'I hardly dare ask.'

'If I'd known you were going to take so long over it, I'd have left the ice-bucket in the fridge.'

'Too long...?' His smile told her that he knew darn well that wasn't the case. 'I could always hurry things up a bit, next time.'

'Don't you dare. I loved every moment of it. So...you're planning on a *next time*?' Kate pulled herself up on the pillows, taking the glass of wine from him. 'I'd be very disappointed if you weren't.'

'Yes. I'm planning on a *next time*.'

He clinked his glass against hers and took a sip, nodding in approval at her choice of wine. It was another pleasure, watching him here in the candlelight.

'This...is bliss. I could stay here for the next week.' Kate stretched lazily. It was impossible. She knew that. Ethan had to get back in the morning for Sam. They both had jobs to go to and, even if they hadn't, this was still new and there was still a lot for them to work through. But it was a nice fantasy.

'Me too.' He reached for her foot, propping it on his thigh, and Kate felt his thumb on her instep.

'That's nice.' The pressure grew a little harder, his thumb circling on the sensitive skin. The soles of her feet were about the only part of her body that Ethan hadn't already caressed and it seemed that he was intent on rectifying that omission now.

'You like it?'

'I love it.' Kate emptied her glass, sliding towards him. Ethan chuckled, taking the glass from her hand and putting it next to his on the bedside table.

'Oh…sorry.' Condensation had dribbled down onto the foot of the glass and he moved it, reaching to pick something up from underneath it.

He had her diary in his hand and was brushing the ring of moisture from the cover. Kate sat up suddenly, grabbing it from him. 'Don't.'

'There's no damage.' His body was suddenly taut, his eyes questioning. Kate clutched the diary, wishing that she'd just let him brush the water off and put it down again. He wouldn't have opened it. He would never have known that she'd mistakenly left it out in its usual place by the bedside.

'Sorry. It wouldn't matter if there was.' A ring on the cover of her diary. It would actually be quite appropriate. Something that Ethan had left here tonight, which couldn't be rubbed away.

But the spell had been broken. Ethan was clearly wondering why she was clutching the book tightly to her chest and no doubt he was about to ask.

'It's… Usha said it might help to write things down. It's my diary.'

'Was that the homework she gave you when she first saw you?' Ethan nodded slowly, his voice taking on that 'everything's all right' tone.

'Not quite. She suggested I make a dream diary, and I've done that. But I decided I wanted to write something every day as well.' Kate ran her finger along the piece of elastic fixed to the back cover and looped around the front, binding the book closed.

He nodded and then smiled suddenly. 'Put it away now. I want to ask, but if you want to share this with anyone it should be Usha.'

'I'm not sharing it with Usha. This is just for me. I might tell her about some of the things I've written but…not about you.' It seemed suddenly as if talking to someone else about what they'd shared would be a betrayal.

Ethan shrugged. 'It's okay. I'm not going to pretend that I'm not curious, but we both have things to work out. At the moment it's enough for me to know that you're doing it, and I hope that's enough for you too. It's important that you say whatever you need to say to Usha. That's how counselling works.'

'You don't mind?'

'I'd mind a lot more if you ever stopped reaching for the healing you need.' He stretched forward, touching the diary. Kate held on to it tightly, her fingers trembling.

'Trust me, Kate. Give it to me.'

He wouldn't look. Kate relinquished the book, watching as he opened the small drawer of the bedside table. His gaze never left her face as he slipped the book inside, closing the drawer.

What would he say if he read the parts about him? The parts where she'd confided her worries about how she'd fit in to Ethan and Sam's tight family unit. About what place she'd have there, the woman who could never replace Ethan's wife or Sam's mother. The parts where she'd said she wasn't sure she could ever trust any man, not even Ethan.

'I… I decided to write two things each day. The best thing that's happened and the worst.' This was something—an admission that the diary wasn't wholly out of bounds and that one day the things in it might be told.

'That sounds like a good idea. Is it working for you?'

'Yes, it is. I…' Kate shrugged helplessly. She just wasn't ready to tell him any more just yet. 'Thank you, Ethan.'

He nodded, a slow smile working its way across his face. He nodded at the clock that stood by the bed. 'As it's only eleven o'clock, I still have time to figure out something that might be the best thing for Saturday.'

'You're already the best thing that's happened to me today.' In so many ways. It wasn't just the sex, it was the way that Ethan understood her. The way he pushed her towards better things, but didn't ask any more of her than she could cope with.

He chuckled quietly. 'There's always something better.'

Moving towards her, his hand closed over the top of her foot and his thumb reached around to massage her instep once more, this time a little harder, more demanding of a reaction. Kate sighed and then caught her breath as she felt his lips against the inside of her leg, working up from the knee.

'Ethan…' She knew exactly where he was going with this. That delicious state, somewhere in between relaxation and tension which was beyond any words. He did it so well.

There was only now. Only his touch. Everything else faded into soft focus as he ran his tongue along the inside of her thigh.

The bed rocked in response to urgent movement. Kate's eyes snapped open and then she squeezed them shut against the light. Ethan's warmth beside her had suddenly been snatched away and it felt as if he'd taken a part of her with it.

'I'm sorry.' She heard his voice, full of regret and panic. Opening her eyes, she focussed on the clock. She'd set the alarm for seven, and they must have both slept through it.

'I'm so sorry, sweetheart. I have to go.' Ethan had dressed in less time that it had taken her to realise what day it was.

She wanted to grab him, pull him back into bed with her. Tell him that Sam would be okay with his grandparents. Have Ethan make love to her for another hour. But that wasn't possible and, even if it had been, Kate wouldn't have done it. She'd known about this going in, and now was no time to complain.

'It's all right. I know.'

He was already making for the door, and she felt a tightness in her chest, the prelude to tears.

At least he wouldn't see them. He'd be gone in a moment. But Ethan turned, striding back towards the bed.

'I wish I could stay.' He wrapped his arms around her, kissing her forehead.

'I wish you could stay too. But you have to go and get Sam. Go…'

All the tenderness, all the passion from last night, was still in his eyes. One last look, and then he stood. This time he didn't turn back.

Kate heard his footsteps on the stairs and the quiet sound of the front door closing. Outside in the lane, a car engine burst into life.

She reached for her diary, flipping through to find the first blank page. She already knew the best and worst things that could possibly happen to her today.

Best: making love with Ethan.

Kate paused, wondering whether she should elaborate. But that pretty much said it all.

Worst: when he left.

She snapped the diary closed, throwing it down on the bed. Now that she was awake, she might as well get up and get on with the day.

CHAPTER FIFTEEN

KATE LOOKED AT her phone. Ethan had called every day for the last four days, just to talk for half an hour after he'd put Sam to bed, and there was no reason why she shouldn't call him. It was half-past nine and he must be alone by now.

Her hands were shaking as she flipped through her contacts list. Maybe she could call Usha instead. But, although Usha had said she could call at any time, Kate didn't want to disturb her at this time in the evening.

'Ethan?'

'Hey there, beautiful. I was about to call you.'

'Sam's asleep?' Why was she whispering? Probably because Ethan was, but then he had to think about not waking Sam. Last night their whispered conversation had seemed delicious, but tonight it felt as if she was doing something wrong by calling him.

'Yes, finally.' There was a moment's silence on the line. 'Is anything the matter?'

How quickly things changed. On the night she'd been mugged, he'd tried to comfort her and she'd pushed him away. Tonight, she wanted him to hold her, but he couldn't.

'I fell asleep on the sofa. I…had a nightmare.'

'Sweetheart…' Ethan's voice seemed very far away. 'I wish I could be there.'

She wished that too. 'It's okay. I just wanted to hear your voice.'

'I'd rather…' He left the thought unfinished. Ethan knew as well as she did that there was no point in talking about what couldn't happen right now. 'You haven't had a nightmare in a while.'

'Not for a couple of weeks. I thought they'd gone, but this one…it was so real. Much more so than the others.'

'Sometimes it needs to be real. We need to get things out of our system before we can let go of them.'

'You think so?' Maybe she should tell him that she needed him and get that out of her system. But it wouldn't do any good. It would only make Ethan feel guilty for not being able to leave Sam, and Kate feel as if she was clinging to him when she had no business doing so.

'You should talk to Usha about this. But it seems to me that it's a good sign—you're ready to face what's happened to you and feel that fear.'

Kate wasn't so sure she was. 'Okay. Yes, I'll do that….'

'Are you going to be able to get back to sleep tonight?'

'Yes. I feel better for talking to you.'

'I wish I could hold you.'

The problem wasn't a practical one. She could get into her car and drive over to his place. But Ethan couldn't offer that. Tonight he was a father and he couldn't mix that with being her lover.

'We'll save that for when I see you. On Saturday.'

His quiet sigh told Kate that he was as unhappy about this as she was. She should face facts and make the best of them. There was no magic wand with which to wave the situation away.

'Yes. I miss you, Kate.'

That was a start. 'I miss you too. Let's talk about something else, eh?'

Kate hadn't remembered before now. It was as if she'd been pushed and then found herself at the bottom of the steps with nothing in between. But, in her dream, she'd felt herself falling. Felt the terror and the pain each time she hit the metal-edged steps on the way down.

Ethan had done his best to cheer her up, but

only the warm presence of his body next to hers had the power to ward off the chill of her dreams. When she ended the call she felt even more alone than she had when she'd woken up from the nightmare.

She could deal with this. Kate stood up, walking to the mirror over the fireplace, staring at her reflection.

'You've done this before.' She saw her own face take on a stern look. 'Now's no different.'

But it *was* different. Knowing that Ethan was there, but that they couldn't be together, made all the difference. Kate turned away from the mirror, not wanting to get into an argument with her own reflection. Maybe writing it all down in the diary Usha had given her would get this feeling under control.

Ethan became aware that he was tapping his foot when the policeman behind the counter raised his eyebrows and glanced downwards.

'Sorry.' He made an effort to keep his feet still and resorted to staring at the ceiling tiles. Then he tried counting them, but fatigue made the rows swim in front of his eyes. It had been a busy week at work and he'd been up early with Sam. But he'd promised Kate that he'd be here.

Finally, after what seemed like an age, she

appeared, holding a large brown manila envelope. She smiled at the officer behind the counter as he let her through and his rather forbidding demeanour brightened by several degrees.

She grabbed Ethan's arm, leading him through the doors and bundling him down the steps.

'Guess what?'

'I've no idea.' From the look on her face it was something good. 'You've won the police raffle?'

'Better than that.'

'They have some good prizes, you know.'

Kate dug her fingers into his ribs. 'Behave. The guy is pleading guilty.'

'Guilty. Really?' Ethan had kept in touch with Mags and there had been no hint that this might happen.

'Yes. It was unexpected, but apparently they found a load of stuff hidden in the loft at his mum's house. Once they had that, he admitted to all the charges. It's such a relief.'

Ethan smiled. Kate hadn't spoken of being worried about this morning's interview, but he knew it had been preying on her mind.

'What did Mags say? Did you see her?'

'Yes. I didn't expect to because she's so senior. She's nice, isn't she?'

'Yeah, she's very nice. Less so if you happen to break the law.'

'Well, she was very nice to me. She said she was very pleased for us.'

'Right.' He supposed that waiting downstairs for an hour had been a bit of a giveaway and this time Mags had put two and two together and come up with the right answer.

'Did you tell her? About us?'

'No. She is a detective, though.' It might make Ethan feel slightly uneasy that everyone seemed to know about him and Kate, but it wasn't exactly a secret. They just didn't tell very many people about it.

'Anyway…listen!' Kate seemed too excited to bother about that at the moment. 'She explained it all to me and said that he's signed a statement and everything. They have him on more than one count of mugging and some other things as well. He's pleading guilty to everything, in the hope that he gets a more lenient sentence.'

'And how do you feel about that?' Ethan asked.

'Well, if it all goes the way it should, I won't have to testify. I wasn't looking forward to that.'

'True enough. You're sure you don't want your day in court, though?' Ethan knew that some people felt that was part of the healing process.

'No. I know what he did and everyone else knows it too. You know it, don't you?'

'I was there, remember? I know exactly what he did.'

'Then that's what I want. I want it over with, and for the courts to decide what happens to him.' Kate gave a firm little nod.

'Then I'm pleased you got what you wanted.'

Kate was practically skipping down the road and it was a joy to see her so happy. 'Oh, I nearly forgot. This is for Sam.'

'What is it?'

'It's for his show-and-tell at school.'

'His what?'

'It's where they stand up and tell the rest of the class about something.'

'Yes, I know what it is.' Ethan could feel a prickle of unease at the back of his neck. 'I just didn't know he was doing one.'

'You must have just forgotten. He asked me if I could get something from the police station when I came round this morning. So I asked Mags if she had anything suitable for his age group and she gave me this. I'm sure we can find something good amongst it all.'

Something gripped the pit of Ethan's stomach and twisted hard. It was entirely up to Sam if he wanted to ask Kate to get him something for school. But he'd rather his son had asked *him*. The realisation that he possibly had but Ethan had forgotten made him feel even worse. Looking after Sam was his responsibility—not Kate's.

'What?' she asked, taking in his expression. 'I thought you'd be pleased.'

'Yes, I am. Thanks very much.' His own voice echoed in his ears, not sounding very pleased at all.

'Did I overstep? I know I'm just a friend…' She was frowning now, and Ethan knew exactly what the unspoken end of the sentence contained. *I know I'm not his mother.*

'No. It's okay, really.' Ethan took the envelope, resolving to listen more carefully in future. Kate wasn't Sam's mother and she was always very careful never to try to be. This was his fault entirely.

But he couldn't let it go. Ethan had grown used to the juggling act that a demanding job and sole care of a five-year-old entailed and now, with his growing relationship with Kate… He was beginning to wonder if he hadn't stretched himself too thin and that he was in danger of dropping all the balls.

But Kate was too precious for him to give her

up. He just had to hope that she'd understand that he couldn't always be there for her. That he couldn't rush to her side and kiss away her fears when she had a nightmare, however much it tore him in two not to.

'Look, I'm sorry, but I'm afraid I have to—'

She arched an eyebrow. 'Go?' she finished for him. 'You don't have to apologise for needing to be somewhere else. I assume that you do?'

Her understanding didn't make it any easier, because he knew that he was short-changing her. 'Yeah, I do. And I should probably be sorting Sam's show-and-tell out with him as well.'

'Okay. Good.' She smiled and Ethan wondered if she was just making the best of a bad job. 'At least that means I won't embarrass you by celebrating over a coffee with the most embarrassing combination of flavours I can think of.'

A stab of guilt slashed at Ethan's heart. 'You couldn't possibly embarrass me. Caramel, cream and a beautiful woman?'

Kate laughed, and this time she seemed truly happy. 'Go. We'll celebrate together later.'

Ethan watched her go, her step a little lighter as she negotiated her way along the crowded high street. It seemed that they still had a way to go before they could work out a way forward in their relationship, but he wanted to make that journey. All he could hope was that Kate would hang on in there with him while he found his way.

CHAPTER SIXTEEN

WHEN ETHAN WAS there all Kate's doubts disappeared. They lay side by side on a blanket at the top of Summer Hill watching the sky darken. There were plenty of places they could have chosen to go on this balmy Saturday evening, but just being together was the most perfect.

'Are you cold?' Ethan's fingers were entwined with hers and he lifted her hand, pressing it to his lips.

'No. Are you tired?' Kate had noticed the dark rings under Ethan's eyes when she'd seen him that morning at the police station.

'Yep. You make me feel tired and happy, instead of just tired.'

'We'll go home. You can sleep.' Tomorrow seemed a long way away at the moment and all Kate could think about was ending today by curling up with Ethan.

'I don't want to sleep when I'm with you.'

Kate sat up, looking down into his face. 'I'll *make* you sleep.'

'And how are you going to do that?' Ethan grinned suddenly.

'Wait and see.'

'I don't have to get up so early tomorrow.' His lips quirked downwards and Kate wondered what could possibly have got in the way of his morning hug for Sam.

'Is that…good?' The idea of being able to wake lazily with Ethan sounded wonderful.

'Yes, it's good.' He reached up, caressing her cheek. 'My mother's doing a "breakfast in bed" party for Sam. Apparently they'll be busy sitting around in their pyjamas and getting crumbs in the bedclothes until ten thirty. There are going to be games and Mum made it very clear that I'm not invited.'

'That's really sweet.' Kate had wondered whether everyone in his parents' village saw Ethan as just the grieving widower. It seemed that his mother, at least, was open to the idea that he might be ready to move on.

'Yeah. When I dropped Sam off this afternoon, she hustled me into the kitchen and gave me a piece of her mind.'

'And?' Whatever Ethan's mother had said, he was obviously thinking about it carefully. And clearly not entirely in agreement with her.

'She says I'm spreading myself too thin. That it would be better for Sam if I included him a little more in our friendship.' Ethan grinned. 'She's being tactful. She knows it's not just a friendship.'

It sounded like good sense. He *was* spreading himself too thin, trying to keep her in one box and Sam in another.

'What do you think?'

'I think that, if you agree… I'd promised to take Sam for pizza this week—maybe you could tag along with us?'

That wasn't what Kate had envisaged, and she doubted it was what his mother had meant either. 'Tagging along' for a pizza they'd already planned was a little different from Ethan deliberately incorporating her into their lives. But maybe that was asking too much of them both right now. It was her choice to be independent of him, just as much as his.

'Yes, I'd really like that.'

'I would too. And Sam will love it.' He sat up suddenly, as if the discussion had taken them as far as he wanted to go. 'You want to go home, now? I'm intrigued to find out exactly how you're going to send me to sleep…'

Pizza night came and went and it changed nothing. They met up in town, ate and then went their separate ways. But it was a start. Something to build on.

Exactly what was going to happen when Ethan's parents ran out of excuses for Sam to stay the night on Saturdays was anyone's guess. But the super-hero space station seemed some way away from completion still and Kate had almost convinced herself not to worry too much about it. Maybe George was stringing things out to give her and Ethan some time alone.

And now she was trembling with anticipation at the thought of another night with Ethan. She opened the front door, strolling out in the evening sunshine to greet him as he parked his car outside her house.

'Hey there, beautiful.' He put his arms around her shoulders.

'Hello, handsome.' She smiled up at him. Ethan always made her feel beautiful.

He turned a little, flipping the remote to lock his car, and then he frowned, looking at her car, which was parked in the driveway. 'What happened there?'

'Someone rear-ended me.'

'What, with you in the car? Are you all right?'

'Yes, I'm fine. He wasn't going all that fast.' Suddenly Ethan seemed more interested in the back of her car than he was in her, walking over to inspect the damage.

'You're sure? No headaches or anything?'

'No, I'm fine. It was just a bump; it looks a lot worse than it actually was. Come inside.' Kate didn't much want to talk about it.

'And you didn't think to call me?'

Yes, she'd thought about calling him. She'd really wanted to call him, but she'd known he'd be busy with Sam, and the thought of her asking and him not being able to come and fetch her was more than she'd been able to bear. It was better that she didn't venture into that territory at the moment.

'I was all right, Ethan. Someone called an ambulance for the guy in the car behind me, just in case, and the paramedics checked me over too. I was fine. I *am* fine.'

'And you won't let me be the judge of that?'

'No, actually.' Kate tried to brush the comment off. Ethan was just reacting from that part of him that still had the urge to protect. It surfaced from time to time, but he always got over it. '*I'm* the best judge of it.'

He turned away from her, bending down to inspect the damage on her car more closely. 'You really should think about getting a new one, Kate. This one's getting more and more unreliable.'

'Yes, I'm thinking about it. But I'm not entirely sure what that has to do with someone crashing into the back of me when I'm stopped at the lights.'

'No. I suppose not.' He shrugged. 'I'm sorry.'

Kate walked into the house and he followed, shutting the front door behind him. It should all be over and done with, but somehow it wasn't. There was more that Kate wanted to say, and from the looks of it more that Ethan had to say too. The unspoken words hung between them in the silence.

She made tea, taking it out into the garden. Kate plumped herself down at the table on the patio, frustration still simmering on a low boil.

'Look, Kate…' Ethan was making an obvious effort to control his exasperation, standing with his back to her, staring out into the garden. 'I can't do this. I care for you and, well, I know you don't want to hear this, but I can't help worrying about you.'

The aching feeling, wanting him to be there for her but too afraid to ask, was too much to bear. 'You have to trust me, Ethan. You can't be here all the time.'

'I can't help that.' He didn't look round.

'I know you can't. But until you can let me out of that box you have me in, you have to accept that I need to carry on with my life. I don't want to replace Sam's mother. I just want to be there for you both, and I'm prepared to wait for that, but until it happens you can't expect me to rely on you on a part-time basis. That's not how it works.'

He turned. The look of helplessness in his eyes was a death knell to all of Kate's hopes. She'd finally said the things she'd written in her diary and it didn't change anything.

'I know. But it's the way I want it to work.' He sighed.

'You want me to be safe, you want Sam to be safe… They're both good things, but you're stretching yourself too thin. You should concentrate on Sam and let me fend for myself for a while.'

This was what Kate knew how to do, fend for herself. She'd been mistaken in allowing herself to rely on Ethan. He wanted to be the one she could depend on but it was too soon. Too hard for him.

'I don't know how to do that.' Something hardened in his eyes.

'You have to try. Ethan, you need to be with Sam and not me. I can deal with that. I just can't deal with your expectations because they make me want things that I can't have.'

Finally it was clear. They'd tried, but both of them had to change. And neither of them could do it quickly enough to stop them from tearing each other apart in the process.

* * *

It was such a small thing. A dent in the back of Kate's car shouldn't be able to wipe away everything they'd meant to each other in the last few months.

But Ethan knew that it wasn't the dent that was the problem. And Kate was right, she couldn't count on him, because he didn't know yet how to put aside his guilt and be the man she wanted him to be.

'You're right. I care about you, but that's not enough.'

'No, it's not. You have to change. *I* have to change.'

Ethan shook his head. He couldn't believe that he was about to say this, but it was the only thing that made any sense. The only thing that would allow her to heal. And maybe it would allow him to heal as well, but that didn't matter very much to Ethan at the moment.

'Don't ever change, Kate. Just find your strength.' He walked past her, trying not to look at her, but his gaze automatically found hers. 'I have to go.'

Her hand flew to her mouth and tears brimmed in her eyes. But she didn't stop him. Ethan walked back into the kitchen, hearing her footsteps behind him as he opened the front door.

'Ethan!' she called out to him and he turned. In that moment, he loved her enough to leave her.

'If you honestly think we can work this out, then tell me now.'

She stared at him wordlessly. She didn't need to say it. Her tears were eloquent enough.

'Then I'm sorry, Kate.'

He opened the front door without waiting for her answer. As he closed the door behind him and walked away, Ethan wished that somehow there could be an answer to all of this. But some things just didn't have an answer.

CHAPTER SEVENTEEN

'WOULD YOU LIKE to take Arthur up to Summer Hill this morning?' Sam was sitting at the table in the conservatory, surreptitiously trying to feed some of his breakfast to the dog.

'Yesss!'

'Good. Well, you'd better make sure that you eat all your breakfast. And that Arthur eats all of his.'

It had been three months and Arthur was growing. The long days of summer had begun to to draw back in again, although the days were still warm. But it seemed to Ethan that he had hardly felt the sun on his face since the evening he'd walked out on Kate.

It was for the best. He'd told himself that so many times now, in an attempt to put the yearning for her back into perspective, that it wasn't necessary to repeat it once again. She was everything he wanted but there was one fatal flaw in their relationship—two, maybe. He was one of the flaws and she was the other.

The doorbell rang and he went to answer it. Sam scrambled down from his seat and followed him.

'What's that?' Sam eyed the parcel that the courier had just handed him.

'I don't know. Probably something from the hospital.'

Sam lost interest, running upstairs, and Ethan called after him. 'I'll be up in a minute.'

But he wasn't. The package contained a hard-bound notebook that he recognised immediately, with a sheet of notepaper slipped under the elastic closure. The world suddenly changed its focus.

Slowly he unfolded the paper. There wasn't much to read.

Dear Ethan
I started this for myself, and now it's for you. You can do whatever you want with it—read it, keep it or destroy it. But I want you to know that you left me better than you found me.
Kate

Ethan stared at the note, trying to divine the meaning behind her words. The writing wasn't

Kate's usual ebullient scrawl, it was neat and careful. She'd obviously thought about what she wanted to say and said it in as few words as possible. And the ending said it all. Just *Kate* without any love or the usual hug and kisses.

If this was a goodbye, he didn't want to read it. They'd already done that and there was no point in opening old wounds. He put the book down on the hall table and then picked it up again, snapping the elastic back and opening it. Kate had sent this to him, wanting him to read it, and there was no way that he could deny her this one last thing.

The pages were closely written and as he flipped through them he saw that she'd almost filled the notebook. It would take a while to read all of this.

'Dad. Come *on*!' Sam's voice sounded from upstairs and for a moment Ethan considered laying the book to one side until Sam was in bed tonight. Then he changed his mind.

'Okay. I'll race you. See who can get ready to go first!'

Getting Sam dressed, chivvying boy and puppy into the car and driving to Summer Hill took less than three quarters of an hour, but it felt like an eternity. Kate's notebook seemed to be burning a hole in the pocket of his jacket. Ethan trudged up the hill, Sam on his shoulders and Arthur trailing behind them on the lead.

Finally they were at the top. Ethan picked a spot where he could keep hold of Arthur's extending lead and Sam could run and play without straying out of sight. He sat down, taking the book from his pocket.

'Can we go to the stream?' Sam was cavorting around in the sunshine.

'Later, maybe. I have to read this…'

Sam puffed out a breath, laying his hand on Ethan's knee in a meditative gesture that seemed somehow older than his years. 'You're getting quite boring.'

Guilt stabbed at Ethan. Sam was right and he wished that he hadn't let his son see his unhappiness. He folded the boy in his arms, hugging him.

'I know. I'm sorry. Can you do something for me?'

'Okay.'

'Would you be able to play for a while, with Arthur, while I read this? I'll be as quick as I can. Then I promise you I'll do my best not to be boring any more.'

Sam nodded gravely. 'All right, then.'

It was so easy for Sam. He believed that his father could say something and then make it happen. As he watched the boy run over to Arthur, Ethan resolved that he *would* make it happen. He'd read what Kate had to say and then get on with his life.

The dates were entered at the top of each page, and underneath were the two entries for each date. Ethan flipped through the pages, stopping at one which contained only two sentences. He recognised the date. It was the day after the second night they'd spent together.

Best: making love with Ethan.
Worst: when he left.

Remorse stabbed at him. He remembered leaving in a hurry, and Kate must have written this then. He almost put the book aside, knowing that it would deal more blows than he could take, but he picked it up again. Kate wouldn't send him this out of spite. She wanted him to read it and he should start at the beginning.

The first pages were dated a few days after she'd started seeing Usha and the entries were hesitant. A cup of her favourite coffee, which made Ethan smile at the memory of Kate grinning and taking a sip. A long evening at the surgery, which had worn her out. But then the entries became more personal.

It was the story of their affair. Brief, shining,

but dogged by doubt. And then the story of her life after that.

Seeing him from her car, heading towards the market in town with Sam on his shoulders. Ethan remembered that day, and wished that he'd turned to see Kate. A nightmare, where someone grabbed her and she fought for her life against a shadow in the night. He smiled at the entries for that day. The nightmare was the worst thing that had happened to her. The best was that it had been a whole month since she'd had that dream.

Being bitten by a dog. The everyday things that Kate had dealt with and then moved on from. There was the recurring theme of missing him, which echoed in Ethan's heart, because he'd been missing Kate too. And the mantra which he now realised that they'd shared for this last three months.

It was for the best. It never would have worked.

And then the tone began to change.

Ethan's the best man I've ever known. He's the one I wanted to depend on, who I knew I could *depend on if we'd just give it a chance. But our fears got in the way.*

I'm learning to face my fears and I hope he can face his.

He knew. It suddenly all seemed so simple

that Ethan couldn't believe he hadn't seen it before. Perhaps he *had* seen it. He'd just been unable to trust enough to do anything about it. Ethan read to the last entry, written the day before yesterday.

I hope that Ethan can understand. I believe he will.

He shut the book with a snap and looked up to where Sam was sitting on the grass, deep in a rather one-sided conversation with Arthur. He understood. Finally, he understood exactly what he had to do.

'Sam. We've got to go.'

'Where?' Sam looked up at him. If his son could trust him to make things right, if Kate could trust him to understand, then what right had Ethan not to trust himself?

'We're going to see Kate. You remember Kate?'

'*I* remember Kate.' Sam shot him a look of reproach. Ethan hadn't spoken about Kate for the last few months and he supposed he deserved that. 'Are we going now?'

'Yes. We're going now.'

Work was the only thing that quietened Kate's mind right now. Hard, physical work. She'd thought a lot about sending her diary to Ethan and in the end the decision had been all about putting an end to missing him and moving on.

But moving on wasn't just something you did whenever you decided to. Telling herself that she'd said all that she wanted to say and that was an end to it didn't stop the endless reworking in her mind. The endless other possibilities that she knew weren't going to happen.

The truth now was that she got on with her life. Maybe he'd send some kind of acknowledgement and maybe not, but knowing Ethan he'd think before he acted. Which meant that, if his reply was coming, it wouldn't be today. Or tomorrow, either.

Large, heavy rocks were just the thing. Maybe she should split a few in half, and add a ball and chain just to complete the effect. She wandered into the kitchen, surveying the pile of built-up earth at the end of the garden, which already boasted the four rocks at the corners which were the basis of her design.

Sweat trickled from the nape of her neck down to the top of her sleeveless vest. She took a bottle of lemonade from the fridge, pouring herself a glass. With any luck, this should take the whole weekend.

The doorbell rang and she dropped the glass in the sink. It smashed, sending shards flying across the draining board, and Kate cursed quietly to herself. When the work stopped, she was jumpier than she thought.

Drying her hands with a tea towel, she opened the door. For a moment, she thought she might be hallucinating.

Ethan was standing at the end of the path looking cool and incredibly handsome. Kate's hand automatically flew to her hair as she watched Sam run up the path towards her, arms outstretched in an impression of an aeroplane.

Shakily she bent down, unable to tear her gaze from Ethan's face. He wasn't smiling, but then again he wasn't *not* smiling. Maybe he felt as awkward as she did, but he certainly looked a lot better.

'What's this, Sam? Are you a plane?' She couldn't think of anything else to say.

'I'm a wing man.'

'Oh.' She was vaguely aware that Ethan was wincing in uneasy embarrassment. 'Do you know what a wing man is?'

'No.' Sam ran in a small circle, his arms outstretched. 'Someone with wings, I think.'

'That sounds about right.' She couldn't stop trembling. Ethan had come, and she didn't know what this meant. But if Sam was with him then surely it couldn't be anything other than a social visit? Maybe an attempt at friendship? Kate didn't quite know how she would respond to that yet.

'Go tell your dad to come here.' She smiled down at Sam, who obligingly veered back down the path, chanting the words at Ethan as he went. He nodded, walking up the path and stopping outside the porch, his fingers on Sam's shoulders.

'I got the book, Kate. And… I was going to come alone, maybe this evening, and then I thought that…' He shrugged. 'Sam and I come as a package. It's a "two for the price of one" deal.'

She didn't dare jump to any conclusions. But Ethan was here and maybe it was a chance to build a few bridges. Kate was covered in grime and sweat, but now was the time.

'Why don't you both come in?' She stood back from the doorway and Sam ran inside. Ethan followed him at a rather more deliberate pace.

'Why are you so dirty?' Sam looked up at her.

'I'm making something in my garden. Do you want to see?' She shepherded Sam through to the back door, looking out for any broken glass that might be on the floor and hoping that Ethan wouldn't notice the sink.

'Wow…it's a castle!'

'It's a rockery, Sam.' Ethan's voice came from behind her. 'Kate's going to plant flowers.'

Sam looked up at her questioningly. 'It's going to be a castle with flowers. What do you think?' Kate provided a compromise answer.

'They're *very* heavy.' Sam was looking at the pile of rocks which had been delivered last weekend.

'Yes, they are a bit.'

'We could give you a hand.'

'You can't, Dad. You've got your best shirt on.' Sam reprimanded him and then looked up at Kate. 'We had to go home so he could put his best shirt on.'

Ethan laughed suddenly as if, faced by an immovable force, he'd decided to give in gracefully. 'What would I do without my wing man to keep me honest?'

Sam shrugged, clearly more interested in the castle than a conversation that he didn't quite understand. He ran across the lawn to inspect Kate's handiwork and Ethan turned to her.

'Kate, I heard what you said. I'm hoping that some of your courage might rub off on me.'

'You mean…?' Suddenly she knew what he meant. It was in the deep-blue gaze that she'd been trying to avoid.

'We both thought we couldn't make things work because we didn't trust ourselves to change. But you've done it and I want to show you that I can too. If you'll give me the chance.

'You think my good intentions will rub off?' She allowed herself a smile at the thought.

'I think they will. Kate, I love you. I want us all to be together—you, me and Sam. If you'll take us.' He shrugged. 'Personally, I'd advise anyone against it. But I'm hoping that you're that reckless.'

She loved him. More than she had before. However successful she'd been in denying it, this had all been for Ethan. For herself as well, but in her darkest moments, when she'd woken frightened in the night, it had been him she'd thought about.

'I love you too, Ethan. I want to give this another try.'

He nodded. His hand wandered to her arm, his fingers leaving a trail of goose bumps. He glanced out at Sam, who was exploring the end of the garden, and then pulled her towards him.

'We'll take care of each other. That has to be enough, doesn't it?'

'It's more than enough. It's everything.' Kate kissed him. It wasn't the deepest of kisses, or the warmest of embraces, but she could feel the shock of sudden pleasure run through him, just as it raced through her.

'You just changed my whole world, Kate.

Tipped it upside down.' He didn't seem to mind that she'd get his best shirt dirty if they went on like this. Holding her close now, he kissed her again.

'Sam...' Kate came to her senses, digging Ethan hard in the ribs. Sam was still exploring the garden, but any moment now he was going to be running back to the house, wanting to share something with his dad.

'I'll explain things to him.' Ethan kept hold of her hand, as if it belonged to him now, and he wasn't going to give it up. 'Or *we'll* explain things. I dare say he'll have a few questions.'

A bright belief in a future that could be different. One that might hold a few problems, but problems were there to be solved.

'And I dare say we can answer them.'

'I think we can. And, in the meantime, it looks as if you have *two* volunteers to help with your new castle.' Ethan nodded towards Sam, who was collecting small stones from the flower beds and piling them up around the larger ones.

'That's good. I could do with the help.'

Ethan had stripped off his shirt, and Sam had followed suit, draping his shirt over his father's. The twitch of Ethan's eyebrow made Kate shiver at the thought that later he might strip off *her* shirt.

They moved the larger rocks together, Ethan issuing a stern instruction to Sam to stand back. He was stronger than she was, but there was equal effort from both of them. Each played their part, instead of Ethan insisting that Kate join Sam and watch.

She was working now because she couldn't stay still. By the end of the day, the rockery was looking more or less as she'd imagined it would, with the added bonus of a few additions of carefully piled pebbles from Sam.

'Chinese?' Ethan straightened up, surveying their handiwork.

'Yes!' Sam liked the idea and Kate grinned.

'Sounds good. I'll get cleaned up.'

He caught her arm, stopping her. Over the course of the afternoon, they'd touched often, but always as a result of heaving rocks or digging holes. Now his fingers on her arm were electric.

'Would you like to come over to mine? Bring a change of clothes. You can clean up there.'

He mouthed one silent word. *Stay*. Kate nodded.

Yes. Whatever the future decided to throw at them, she'd stay.

Blind trust had been Ethan's only weapon against the fears that today had brought into sharp focus. What if Kate didn't want him? What if it was all too late and her diary really was a sign that she'd moved on? As soon as that fear had been assuaged, two new ones had replaced it.

What if Sam didn't understand? And what if Ethan was in too deep and he couldn't do what he'd promised and change?

Sam had turned out to be the least of his problems. He'd sat down with him after dinner, told him that he loved him and that he'd always be his wing man. And that Daddy and Kate wanted to go out together. Sam had nodded sagely.

'I know about boyfriends and girlfriends. You want to kiss her, don't you?'

Ethan wondered vaguely what else Sam knew and decided to leave that one for another time. 'Yes. I do.'

Sam turned the corners of his mouth down and Ethan's heart thumped, wondering what was going on in Sam's head. Then he slithered down from Ethan's lap, running over to Kate.

'Can we have ice cream—in the castle again?' When the afternoon had been at its warmest, Kate had predictably resorted to ice cream, eaten perched on the rocks in the rockery.

'Yes, of course. In fact, that's one of the rules. We can have ice cream in the castle whenever you want.'

Ethan decided not to intervene. Kate's idea of ice cream whenever you wanted was tempered by a balanced diet in between times, while Sam's wasn't. That was a minor detail that could be sorted out later. Sam's smile was the one thing that could make things complete at the moment.

And he did smile. Kate hugged him and he clambered up onto her lap. 'Do you know the story?'

Her gaze flipped to Ethan's face, and he grinned. Surely happiness couldn't be *this* easy? 'I'll fetch the book. Would you like Kate to read your bedtime story?'

Sam nodded, and Kate hugged him tight, her face shining. 'Get the book, Ethan.'

When they'd both kissed Sam goodnight and Ethan had put him to bed, the second fear resurfaced. He and Kate were alone now and he had to live up to all he'd promised. He almost didn't dare touch her.

'I meant what I said, Kate. I'm going to let go of the guilt. I'm going to be there when you need me.' How he was going to do that was a question that still baffled Ethan. But he *would* do it.

'I trust that you will be.' She stepped into his arms and Ethan felt his heart thump in his chest. 'And I'll be there for you and Sam.'

It felt so good to hear her say that. The suspicion that Kate might just have the answer for everything occurred to him.

'And if I start falling back into my old ways, you'll tell me?'

'I'll do a lot more than tell you…' She jabbed him in the ribs.

'Always?'

'Yes, always.'

Always was more than he deserved, and more than he'd ever thought possible. Ethan would take it.

'Come to bed.' He wanted Kate in his arms more than anything now.

'I thought you'd never ask…'

EPILOGUE

Six months later.

THEY'D SEEN THE last of the hot summer days and the beginning of autumn, the sparkle of Christmas and bright new hope for the coming year.

Things hadn't always been easy. Kate had worked hard to make Sam feel that she wasn't taking his father from him and that she wasn't trying to replace his mother. But Sam, already secure in the knowledge that his father loved him, had come up with his own answer. His mother was 'Mummy' and, after a few months, he'd started to call Kate 'Mum'. When Kate had taken him to buy a Christmas present for Ethan, Sam had revelled in having a secret to keep and someone else to keep it with.

The evening she'd come home late from work and found Ethan pacing the sitting room had brought back all Kate's old fears. The silence between them had lasted for a while and then

Ethan had simply walked up to her and hugged her. She'd felt his tears, wet against her face, and they'd talked for hours. His darkest fears and hers were finally seeing the light of day, where they could at last be calmed.

When she'd moved into Ethan's house, she'd kept most of the boxes she'd brought with her packed, not wanting to disturb anything that Jenna might have done. Her cottage was closed up, all the furniture under dust sheets, because Kate could quite bring herself to rent it out yet. Ethan had said nothing for a week and then, when Kate had returned home from a shopping trip with his mother, she'd found that everything had been moved. Cutlery was in a different drawer, plates were in a different cupboard. The furniture was in a different place in their bedroom and Kate's things had been neatly packed away in drawers and cabinets. The relief was tempered by neither of them being able to find anything for weeks.

Ethan had organised a surprise, a visit to London with a stay in a luxurious hotel. Just the two of them, while Sam stayed with Ethan's parents. They had breakfast in the huge bed and then a walk in the crisp, winter morning.

'Is this the place?' He stopped suddenly, right

next to the statue of Boudicca that looked out over the Thames.

'You remembered!' Kate smiled up at him.

'Your second-favourite place.' He wrapped his arms around her. They were both secure in the knowledge that being in each other's arms was their shared favourite place.

'Yes. Even in winter I like it.'

He was looking up at the statue. 'Think Boudicca had red hair—like you?'

Kate laughed. 'I have absolutely no idea. I wouldn't mind the chariot, though.'

'Sam and I could take a look at your car. I'm sure we could do something with it.' Ethan grinned, shoving his hands in the pockets of his coat, his breath pluming in front of him in the cold air.

'Is this…was there something you wanted to mention?' Kate was going to wait, and pretend she knew nothing about any surprise, but he seemed so on edge all of a sudden and it seemed downright cruel not to put Ethan out of his misery.

He winced. 'Sam told you, didn't he?'

'No, he didn't. When you were taking his things inside at your parents' house he sat in the car, looking at me with his hands over his mouth. I asked him if anything was the matter, and he said that he'd promised you not to tell.

He says that, now that he's six, he's grown up enough to keep a secret.'

Ethan laughed. 'Do you mind? That he's in on it?'

'Of course not. He's your wing man, isn't he?'

They'd talked about going away somewhere for Easter and Kate had come to the conclusion that Ethan must have tickets in his pocket.

'Yes. I might have to have a word with him about strategy…' Ethan wound his arms around her shoulders, kissing her.

'Mmm. Lovely. Can we go now? I'm getting cold,' she teased him.

'No, stay right there. Don't move an inch.'

He dropped to one knee in front of her and Kate's hand flew to her mouth. *This* she hadn't expected.

'What…? Ethan!' She was trembling all over now, hardly able to stand. 'I thought you'd booked a weekend away.'

He smiled. 'I want more than a weekend. I'm aiming for the rest of our lives. Will you marry me, Kate?'

She might not have expected the question, but she had her answer ready. 'Yes. Yes, I will!'

He got to his feet and kissed her. Kate was dimly aware of the city going about its business around her. That a few people had stopped when they'd seen Ethan down on one knee and that when he'd kissed her there was a murmur of approval. A woman's voice came from somewhere, wishing her happiness. She nodded blindly. Ethan was the only thing she could see right now.

'You'll be relieved to hear that I didn't take any of my wing man's advice on choosing the ring.'

'You have a *ring*?' Here in his arms, that hardly mattered. All that mattered was that Ethan wanted to spend his life with her, and she wanted so much to spend the rest of her life with him.

'Of course I do. I've got a plan.' He took a small box from his pocket, opening it and showing Kate the contents. 'Do you like it?'

It was a square-cut canary-yellow diamond on a plain white-gold band. Kate caught her breath. 'It's beautiful, Ethan.'

'Let's see whether it fits. Hold still. Stop jumping around.'

'I can't help it!' Kate's feet seemed to be doing a little dance of excitement, quite of their own volition and without any input from her.

He slid the ring onto her finger, pushing it carefully over the knuckle. It was a perfect fit and Ethan nodded in satisfaction. 'Not so bad. I was hoping that I'd got it right.'

'It's perfect, Ethan. Beautiful… How *did* you get it right?'

'I measured your finger while you were asleep. Ticklish business. I was hoping you weren't going to wake up and catch me doing it.'

Kate laughed with delight. 'It was a beautiful plan, Ethan. Thank you so much.' She flung her arms around his neck, hugging him.

'There's more.'

'I don't care. This is enough, and nothing you could possibly do could be any better.'

He laughed, a low rumble of complete contentment. 'Try this…'

He handed her an envelope and Kate opened it. It was a letter from a firm of land surveyors. She scanned the words, too excited to read them the first time, and tried again.

He'd made an offer on the land adjacent to her cottage. One acre, with planning permission to build. Kate flipped over to the next page and saw a plan. The land included the old orchard that she could see from her back window, and extended to the side right up to the curve in the lane.

'This is… But aren't we going to rent the cottage? What does it mean?'

'It means that, if we want to, we can take your cottage off the rental listings and extend it. Very considerably, actually, as the planning permission allows us to double the frontage and go back to form an L-shape. It would give us three times the space you have now.' He turned the page in front of her and Kate saw a plan of the new building, which ran along the side of her cottage, reaching almost to the end of the garden. 'The planning authorities say that the frontage would have to be in a complementary style, but then I think we might want that anyway.'

'But we can't afford this, can we? Have we won the lottery or something?'

Ethan chuckled. 'No. We'll sell my house.'

'No… Ethan, how things are at the moment is fine. You don't have to sell up.'

'It's just a house, Kate. I like it, but this would be something that we'd built together. There's a great little school in the village for Sam. And we'd have space.'

'For Sam to grow. And…more children?' Kate put her arms around his waist.

He smiled broadly. 'That possibility hadn't escaped me. Along with Arthur, and a few cats and dogs, and whatever else you bring back from the surgery needing a temporary home. You'll keep your garden, and I can grow apple trees.'

'You've got this all worked out, haven't you?'

'It's nothing without you, Kate. If this isn't what you want, then we'll do something else. I have a week to sign the documents on the land, but if I do it's ours.'

'You're sure this is what you want?' It sounded like heaven, but if Ethan wanted to live in a shack she'd be fine with that too.

He took her hand, kissing it, and the ring flashed in the winter sunlight. 'You've got your own Ambigulon stone. You could try it out.'

'Is that what Sam said?'

'Yeah. Although that wasn't anywhere on the list of priorities when I chose it.'

'Might come in handy, though…' She held her hand over his heart. 'I see… Ah. It's all good.'

Ethan chuckled. 'You can't stop there. What *do* you see?'

'I see an honest heart that loves me as much as I love you, Ethan. I think your plan is just perfect.'

'I'm glad you like it.' He put his arm around her and started walking. He was holding her tight, guiding her steps, because Kate wasn't looking where she was going. All she could see was the ring on her finger and the man she was going to marry.

'It'll keep us busy. A wedding and a house. Children…'

'They'll keep us very busy. But there are a few other things in the plan as well.'

'Hot chocolate?' She grinned up at him and he nodded. 'Happy for the rest of our lives?'

'Yes. The first is about ten minutes' walk away. The second starts right now.'

* * * * *

If you enjoyed this story,
check out these other great reads from
Annie Claydon

FORBIDDEN NIGHT WITH THE DUKE
SAVING BABY AMY
ENGLISH ROSE FOR THE SICILIAN DOC
THE DOCTOR'S DIAMOND PROPOSAL

All available now!